Burn Baby Burn

A dark steamy retelling of Cinderella

Miranda Grant

Burn Baby Burn

This is mostly a work of fiction. UK places, historical timelines, and cultural information are based on what research I could find. The characters and incidents are all products of my imagination and should not be seen as having any more credibility than fake news does. Any resemblance to actual events, locales, organizations, or persons, living, dead, or stuck in purgatory, is entirely coincidental.

Then again…very little is known about what really happened back in the day, so who can say for sure?

Chapter header font by Renn Crump. Subtitle font by George Williams.

Cover and inside artwork by Jamie Dalton at Magnetras Book Covers.

BY MIRANDA GRANT

WAR OF THE MYTH SERIES

Elemental Claim
Think of Me Demon
Tricked Into It
Rage for Her

FAIRYTALES OF THE MYTH STANDALONES

Burn Baby Burn

Hey, you. Yeah, you:

Let's make a superhero team.

Meetings on Tuesday?

Pronunciation Guide

Characters

Aurelia................Aw-rail-lee-uh
Cadeyrn................Kay-der-in
Daman.............Day-men
Felix ....Fee-licks
Fionnghula ....Fehn-ooh-la
Flavia.............Flah-vee-uh
Ignis................Ig-neice
Octavia.............Oct-tay-vee-uh
Rekzor ....Rike-zer

Places

Caledonia.............Cal-lee-doe-nee-uh
Derventio ....Der-vin-she-o
Gaera.............Guy-ear-ruh
Luguwalos................Loo-guh-wah-lus
Pyveelv............ Pie-vee-elv
Selgovae.................Sel-go-vee
Novantae.............No-vahn-tay

Characters

Fionnghula (Ella) – A child of the Novantae clan. When her village is raided by the Selgovae, she's captured and sold as a slave to the Romans.

Cadeyrn – A child of the Novantae clan. He's three years older than Ella and has been her arch nemesis all her life. When his village is raided by the Selgovae, he's captured and sold as a slave to the Romans.

Daman Tar – A dark fae with a vendetta and too much time on his hands. His plans for Ella involve much more than just getting the emperor's son to fall in love with her…

Felix – Emperor Hadrian's son. He's a strong warrior and has been sent up to squash the Caledonia uprising on the northern border of the Roman Empire.

Octavia – A perfectionist Roman housewife who is not above getting her hands dirty in order to get what she wants.

Aurelia – Octavia's eldest daughter. A soft heart on the outside. A cruel, manipulative bitch on the inside.

Flavia – Octavia's youngest daughter. Crueler than her mother and sister, she enjoys punishing Ella every chance she gets.

Caledonia

Selgovae

Novantae

Tyrron Doon

Brigantes

Turf Wall

Luguwalos

Elva Hill

Derventio

Brocavum

Ravenglass

Roman Empire

N

S

E

W

50km [1 day's journey]

hapters

Prologue

The Birth of a Queen
3568, Dyveelv, Caera (102 on Earth)

"By the gods, woman! I'm not blind! I can see that she's not mine!" King Rekzor roared, pointing furiously at the babe in his wife's arms. "That — that *thing* is an abomination!"

Crimson eyes flashing, Queen Ignis met his fury with the hot blaze of her own. "Abomination or not, she is *our* daughter!" The 'our' was stressed so fiercely that Rekzor could only stare in gaping silence.

How could she be dumb enough to think that he would believe her? The evidence of her infidelity was staring him right in the face! No child of his would have blue eyes. He was a fire elementalist, born into one of the oldest clans. Red eyes had been dominant in his family for millennia – as they had been in his wife's line! For the babe to have blue eyes, the bitch must have cheated.

Rekzor growled. He had half the mind to strangle her before she could regain her strength. But the other half, blast it, was still madly in love with her. Even when faced with solid proof, the king couldn't bring himself to punish his queen. Gods know why; she fucking deserved it.

Snarling, he shook his head in disgust and turned away. He couldn't look at them for a moment longer. Her eyes pleaded with him, while the baby's called him a fool.

Stalking to the door, Rekzor addressed not his queen, but the midwife.

"There was no joy here, tonight," he snapped. "Do you understand? Our baby was born without breath."

"Rekzor!" Queen Ignis shouted.

Turning, he created a ball of fire in his hand. His eyes were as dark as his soul, expressing the depth of his anger. "Shall I burn it now? Shall I toss this ball at its head?"

He was spitting with fury. His heart was breaking. He hated that fucking babe.

And yet, his wife had the audacity to pull the bastard tighter to her chest. "You will do no such thing! She is our daughter!"

"She is no daughter of mine!" The fireball got hotter, brighter. It twisted with his pain, fed on the anger boiling inside him. "She has blue eyes!" he roared. "She'll have the power of water – an ability neither of us possess!"

"I did not sleep with a water elementalist!" Queen Ignis' entire body flushed, her skin burning with the force of her own rage. She was one of the very few fire elementalists with the ability to turn her whole body into a weapon. Most, like he, could only control it through their hands. But he'd hope their child…

"Do not lie to me!" If he threw the ball, Ignis wouldn't be hurt. The babe would though. It would cook alive, not yet old enough to smother its flames. Oh gods, was he tempted.

"Don't you dare," she growled. The baby started to cry, the room getting too hot for its fragile flesh.

King Rekzor sneered in disgust. Still, he could not bring himself to kill the babe. Ignis would never forgive him.

He sucked in a harsh breath at that, wanting so much to scream. She should be the one begging for his forgiveness. She was the one that had robbed him of an heir by sleeping with a fucking water elementalist! She was the one who had broken his trust, who had broken his heart.

Shaking his head, he closed his fist. The flames snuffed out as if they'd never been. "Get rid of it tonight. Throw it into the human realm if you have to," the king ordered. "Or I swear upon Awryn's last breath, I will burn the bastard alive."

Not waiting for an answer, Rekzor stalked into the hall and slammed the door shut behind him. He waited until he'd rounded the corner before dropping to his knees. With a heart-wrenching scream, he threw his arms out wide. Fire erupted from his palms, licking down the hall in testament to his anger and pain.

He didn't stop until he heard it – the solemn tolling of bells. Breathing deeply, he then dropped his arms to his sides. Fire no longer poured from his palms, no longer screamed of his agony. For the bells had a message, the most beautiful message of them all: the bastard was dead.

Chapter One

And So It Begins
112 Caledonia (Scotland, Earth)

"Ye own parents didn't want ye! They left ye out in the woods to die as a babe. Everyone knows the tale!" Cadeyrn taunted as he shoved Ella to the ground. He looked around his group of friends, a leer stretched across his lips. "I bet her mother was a Roman whore!" he shouted.

Cruel laughter sang out all around her. Ella's cheeks began to burn as she dug her nails into the damp earth. With a growl, she jumped to her feet and swung. Her fist connected with Cadeyrn's jaw.

"Ye whore!" Snarling, he lunged for her.

Ella braced herself, her eyes flashing fire. She knew how to fight. She had five brothers, after all. They might not be related by blood as Cadeyrn claimed, but they'd taught her how to throw a punch.

With a fierce yell, Ella twisted to the side. The boy's momentum had him sailing past her, too fast to stop. She shoved him hard, knocking him off his feet. His angry sneer turned into a slackened jaw. His eyes widened as he crashed to the ground, arms flailing. Ella jumped on top of him, her little fists swinging. She grunted with each hit. Pain shot up her arms, but she did not stop.

Cadeyrn was twice her size and the blacksmith's son. She couldn't let him regain his wits and hit her back. But even as she raised a hand for another punch, he bucked beneath her. She flailed, her eyes growing wide. She tried to scramble off him, but he yanked on her ankle and rolled her beneath him.

Fighting her wild swings, he grabbed at her hands. She twisted as much as she could, rubbing her skin raw, but eventually he managed to pin her. His chest heaved. His face was heavily bruised. Blood ran down his nose and mouth. One eye was swollen. The other was a thin slit of anger.

Growling, Ella promptly spat in his face.

He raised a fist high above him, his glare threatening severe retribution.

Meeting his scowl, Ella refused to cower. She knew how to give a punch and she knew how to take one.

"I'm going to kill ye," he sneered.

"A lot of talk for a boy that can barely see!" And then she swung at him again because like a fool, he'd released her wrists to get in a shot of his own.

Screaming, he hit her. Pain exploded in her face. Her head snapped sideways. Her teeth ripped into the inside of her cheek. Blood stained her lips and ran down her chin. The next blow closed one of her eyes. Now they were like two matching dolls and that just pissed her off.

Grabbing a handful of dirt, Ella threw it at his face. He cursed as it went into his one good eye. Taking advantage of his momentary blindness, she shoved him off her and jumped to her feet.

She tried to make a tactical retreat, but Cadeyrn's group of friends closed in around her. They shoved her back and forth until their leader could see again. When he grabbed her from behind, she sent an elbow into his ribs.

"What are ye fighting over now?" a man roared.

The crowd instantly dispersed, the boys vanishing into the trees. Cadeyrn held Ella pinned to his chest, an arm wrapped around her throat. His grip relaxed at the sight of her father. Dropping his arm, he quickly stepped away.

"We were just playing," he mumbled, looking down at the ground.

"Just playing? Ye eye is swollen shut!"

Ella grinned smugly.

"And ye!" Her grin promptly disappeared. "What have I told ye about picking fights? Ye are about to be a woman soon. Ye can't go beating people up. No one will want to marry ye then."

"I'm never marrying!" Ella said stubbornly. "I'm going to be a warrior like ye!"

He raised his blue eyes to the sky. "Rhiannon give me strength," he muttered. Looking back down, he deepened his scowl. "We have discussed this. Ye are a chieftain's daughter, my daughter. Ye will marry either Fergus or Aengus."

"I'd rather marry a frog!"

"Don't tempt me!" he roared.

"It's true! Fergus smells like an ogre and Aengus fights like a girl!"

"Ye're a girl!"

"Aye, well." She crossed her arms, not quite sure what to say to that.

Pinching the bridge of his nose, her father sighed. "We will discuss this later. Right now –"

"So are ye saying that it is up for discussion though?" she cut in hopefully.

He groaned. Shaking his head, he said, "Ye have too much of yer mother's brain in ye, aye."

Ella's smile faltered, but she wrenched it back up. She didn't have anything of Artula in her. As Cadeyrn had so cruelly reminded her, she was not their child.

"But as I was saying, right now, we must discuss yer punishment. Fighting is not to be allowed. And why are ye out so far. Ye know better than to wander past the –" He cut off suddenly, his mouth dropping open, his face turning ashen.

A chorus of screams sounded behind him, but they were soon overtaken by Ella's own.

Her father stumbled forward.

"Fire!" Caderyn shouted, but all Ella could see was the large spear sticking out of her father's back.

"Father!" she cried as she rushed forwards to catch him. But he was too heavy. He crushed her beneath his weight.

"Run," he rasped.

"Nay, I'll not –"

"Take her, Cadeyrn. That's an order."

"Father!" Tears burned her eyes as Cadeyrn grabbed her arm and dragged her out from under their chieftain. She fought him with everything she had, but once he'd lifted her off her feet, there was very little she could do. She was barely ten summers old. He was ten and three and hadn't wasted all of his strength on their fight earlier.

"Father!" she screamed as the boy dragged her further into the woods, away from home. She looked up and finally saw the fire in the distance.

Their village was covered in flames, their wooden huts the perfect kindling. Another spear was tossed in their direction. It slammed into a tree. So close, but she didn't care. Her father was struggling to his feet. He drew the sword he always carried from the scabbard at his waist.

With gritted teeth, he raised his arm over his shoulder and hacked at the wood sticking out of his back. He cried out as that moved the metal inside him. Blood poured to the ground, but he stayed standing. He stayed strong. He was going to be okay. Ella had to believe that.

Three men rushed forwards to meet him.

"Go!" he ordered. Bracing himself, her father raised his sword. He cut down the first man, spun and dodged the second's attack. The third kicked him in the knees. Ella reached down and bit Cadeyrn's arm. Cursing, he dropped her. She lunged forward, pulling out the dagger she'd been given as a gift last summer.

Flinging herself into the fray, she jumped onto the third man's back and stabbed in quick succession. Once, twice before he ripped her off him and tossed her into a tree. She crumbled to the ground. The air left her lungs. It hurt to breathe, but she pulled herself to her knees. She looked up just in time to see the second man slicing at her father. Blood spurted into the air. Hot tears burned her vision. A ghoulish scream ripped from her lungs as he collapsed to his knees.

His sword slipped from his hand.

His eyes found hers.

"No!"

The world blurred. A rough hand yanked her into the air. She kicked and screamed, but it wasn't a boy she was fighting this time.

A fist collided with the side of her skull. Her cries stopped. Cadeyrn took them up, but his were deeper, more focused. He must have charged at the man holding her because she was suddenly dropped to the ground. She whimpered as she looked at her father. His eyes were open, but he no longer saw her.

Choking on a sob, Ella crawled forward. She grabbed one of his hands. It was still warm. He could still come back. She'd heard of the fae being able to heal people from terrible wounds. As long as they were still warm, they could do it.

She just had to get him to the stones.

Desperately, she looked up. Which way was it? She couldn't see the sun through the clouds and smoke and tears. She couldn't –

"No!"

Heavy hands jerked her back. She was dragged along the ground by her hair. Strands ripped free, but not enough to free her. She lost her grip on her father. His eyes stayed watching her. She tried to scream his name, but she couldn't breathe.

She couldn't breathe.

And nor could he.

Chapter Two

For Father

With every step, Ella's heart gave out just a little bit more. She was leaving her father. Her home. Everything she had ever known. It was all disappearing beneath her feet. Everything except Cadeyrn.

He walked beside her in silence, his hands bound in front just like hers. His chin was raised, his shoulders thrust back with pride despite the bruising on his face. Fury hardened his eyes. He hated her. He'd always hated her and now he hated her even more. She could feel his anger radiating off him.

And for some reason that hurt. It hit like a hammer on top of all her other pain. He was all she had left. She was all he had left. Didn't he see that?

Sniffling, Ella wiped her nose on her shoulder. She looked at him beneath her wet lashes, but he looked straight ahead. There wasn't a single tear on his cheek.

Her eyes narrowed. How could he not grieve? How could he not see her father every time he closed his eyes even on the slightest of blinks? How could he not –

"Hey," Cadeyrn said softly.

He nudged her shoulder as an uncontrollable cascade of tears ran down her face. She shook on heavy sobs that she didn't even know she was making.

"Ye are a warrior and warriors doona cry," he said softly.

"I am...no...war...war..." She broke on another sob.

"Ye are." He lowered his voice so the others walking alongside them couldn't hear. "Ye killed that man."

She looked up, her eyes red and swollen. Snot ran into her mouth and down her chin. But it wasn't pain in her heart at the moment. It was anger. Fury. The need for revenge.

That bastard had killed her father. He'd knocked him down so his friend could slice his throat. He'd stolen him from her. He'd taken everything from her.

Ella's fists clenched. Her jaw tightened. "Truly?" she asked.

"Aye. Do ye see him with us? He was here at the start of our trek."

She looked around. A dozen odd men marched beside them, but that bastard was not one of them. She smiled. He had been her first kill. Her eyes landed on his friend.

And he will be my second.

"That's it," Cadeyrn murmured. "Dry ye tears and hold on to ye strength, Fionnghula."

Sniffling, Ella nodded. Her full name was rarely used,

but then Cadeyrn wasn't exactly a friend, now was he? She hated him. Just this morning, they'd bruised each other's eyes and last week they'd busted each other's lips fighting over who was less competitive. He was her number one enemy.

And her only friend.

Wiping her face, she took a deep breath. "Call me Ella," she said, squaring her shoulders.

He hesitated. Then he looked away. After a moment, he nodded. "Keep yer head up, Ella. The gods will see us home."

No, she vowed as they marched on. I *will see us home.*

Ella stayed up all night, watching. Waiting. Her father's killer had hunkered down only a few feet from her. His knife laid beside him. His snores made her smile.

It might not be honourable to kill a man in his sleep, but neither was stabbing a man in the back with a spear. Or fighting him three against one. Her father's killer didn't deserve to die honourably. He deserved to die a fool, killed in his sleep by a wee lass.

Smiling sadistically, Ella turned her attention to the man on guard. He had his back to her, facing westward. Facing the direction of her home. She couldn't help but leer over that. His fears were justified. It would be a Novantae that killed him. She would kill every last one of these men. Either in this life or the next.

Eyes cold, Ella watched as he headed deeper into the woods. He would be gone for only a moment. She had to act fast, though not so fast she alerted the other men around her.

Creeping to her feet, Ella inched over. She bent down slowly. Picked up the knife. It glistened under the full moon. She caught her reflection in the metal.

Wild red hair curled around a face still rounded by youth. Bright blue eyes lay swollen above a row of freckles. She might not yet be a woman, but she was already a warrior. She had taken her first kill this morning. And now she would take her second.

Gripping the knife in her hand, Ella sneered down at the man before her. He was still asleep. Almost peaceful looking. Almost...innocent looking. She swallowed as her hand started to shake.

She could do this. He had killed her father. He had kidnapped her. His men had tied her hands and forced her on an entire day's walk. She hurt so much and it was all because of him.

All she had to do was fall onto his chest. Her weight would drive the knife home. Then she could watch him die, gasping for life just like her father had done. Her chest constricted. The blade shook.

She could do this.

She had to do this.

For her father.

"Ella..."

Bound hands reached forwards and grabbed the knife. Cadeyrn looked at her, but she turned away. She didn't want to see his pity. Warriors did not cry over their kills.

"Go back to bed," he said softly. "The guard will return soon."

She nodded on a shaky exhale. Tears blurred her feet, but she still managed to walk without making a sound.

Laying back down in her spot, Ella curled into a ball of agony.

And then she heard it.

A wet squelch followed by a gurgle.

The deed was done.

Cadeyrn slipped back into his spot. It was too dark to see if there was any blood on him, but the dagger in his hands was unmistakable. Holding his gaze, Ella looked into his cold green eyes. She swallowed, her heart so loud she feared it would wake everyone up.

His voice was gravelly and hoarse as he leaned over and cut her binds. "Wait for the next guard to go away," he whispered. "Then we run."

Ella waited in the dark, praying that the sun was not about to rise. The moon was out, almost full, but there were clouds blocking its light. If they could get away before morning, they would have a chance to hide in the woods. Then they could run home. She could see her brothers again. She could be at her father's burial. Tears misted her eyes.

"Father," she mouthed in pain. It was a word she would never speak again.

"Now, Ella." The urgency in Cadeyrn's voice had her snapping out of her misery. She jumped to her feet, grabbed Cadeyrn's hand, and ran. They dashed into the woods in the opposite direction the guard had gone. The branches whipped at their faces. Cries rang up behind them. Ella tried to run faster, but she tripped over her feet.

She bit her tongue so she wouldn't make a sound when she hit her hip. Her eyes watered. Cadeyrn jerked her to her feet and together, they ran deeper.

Footsteps sounded behind them. Something rustled in

the underbrush. Cadeyrn ran faster, dragging her along behind him. She tried to keep up but stumbled again. Her hand slipped out of his. He ran off, leaving her behind. Her heart hammered wildly as she hit the ground. She could hear the men behind her. They'd found their fallen comrade, his throat slit like an animal's. They wouldn't be kind when they finally got hold of them. She had to run. She had to –

Ella screamed as a hand grabbed her by the shoulder. She was wrenched around. A sneering face filled her vision. His eyes were cold and black. His breath was foul. "That was my son!" he roared.

His fist reared back. She screamed.

Something flew above her, glinting in the moonlight. The man fell back. Gasps and groans escaped his lips. Another hand grabbed her shoulder and wrenched her back.

"Come on!" Cadeyrn urged. He left the dagger behind as he pulled her onward.

But he was too late. The men had them surrounded. Cadeyrn pushed her behind him, rotating with her at his back as he looked in every direction. She could feel his desperation to escape. He was a cornered animal and he would rather die than be recaptured.

As she put her back against his, her heart rate sped up. She didn't want to die. But she didn't want to be a slave either. She knew the fate that would befall them if these men won. Her father had warned her about going too far east. The Selgovae had changed, he'd told her. The war with the Romans had made them desperate. They were no longer their friends. They were slave traders trying to stop their own families from being taken.

"We don't want to hurt ye," one of the Selgovae men

said. His face was familiar. She'd been glancing at him since the start, trying to figure out who he was, but it wasn't until now that it hit her.

"Fial?" she gasped. She'd played with his two sons... They'd broken bread together...

He looked away. The shame on his face a hot arrow to her heart.

Tears burned her eyes. On a bellow of rage, Ella raced forwards and threw herself at him. She kicked and hit at his stomach, but he just wrapped his arms around her and pinned her limbs to her side.

"Stop!" he ordered.

She screamed and bit down on the arms holding her. Blood spurted into her mouth. He shoved her away. She tried to turn around so she could attack him again, but he kicked the back of her knee. She stumbled. Her body twisted. Her foot slipped.

Arms flailing, Ella fell backwards and hit the ground hard. Her head smacked into a rock. The sharp tang of blood permeated the air. The world tilted, then faded.

As her eyes closed, the last thing Ella was aware of was Cadeyrn's scream of rage.

Chapter Three

The Good Life

She woke with a hard shoulder pressed into her chest, a thick arm wrapped around her legs. Her hands were rebound, this time behind her. Her feet were tied too and her head throbbed with a pain that threatened to make her sick. With every step the man took, it jiggled her stomach. Had Ella eaten anything recently, she would've been sick all down his back.

Instead she groaned weakly and turned her head, looking for Cadeyrn.

He watched her with his one swollen eye. Hatred burned in its depths, but at the sight of her awareness, it softened into concern.

"Ye okay?" he whispered.

She blinked slowly. Nodded. Or at least she thought

she had. She wasn't sure about anything anymore. It hurt just to concentrate.

"Father?"

Cadeyrn frowned. He glanced away before looking back.

"Where's father? I want…"

Moisture glistened his eyes. The man holding her sucked in a breath. His grip shifted.

Raising her head weakly, Ella looked up. "Where is…"

She trailed off as reality suddenly came back to her. A tear slipped down her cheek. She clenched her fists. She wanted to scream, but her head hurt too much.

Fighting back the rest of her tears, Ella lifted her head. She couldn't see home through the trees, and the ache in her chest told her she'd never see it again. She'd never see her father. Never play with her brothers. Never hear their laughter nor –

Swallowing hard, she collapsed back down on Fial's shoulder. He shifted her into a more comfortable carry. His hand lingered on her back, almost as if he was trying to apologise. Closing her eyes, Ella fell into her grief.

They walked for a few more hours before arriving in the town of Luguwalos. She was then lowered, the ties on her feet freed so she could hobble alongside them. Cadeyrn watched her, worry in his eyes.

She took her first step and winced, but she didn't fall down. Fial pushed her along. Cadeyrn growled, but the shake of her head stopped him from doing anything more.

They needed to conserve their strength. They would be sold. They would be purchased. Killing Fial and the other Selgovae wouldn't do anything to change that. Someone else would just profit from their loss.

Lifting her chin, Ella walked through the crowded streets. The smell of fresh bread caused her stomach to growl and she instinctively turned towards it. She caught the eye of a woman standing in the doorway of a wooden hut. There was flour on her cheek and pity in her eyes. Scowling, Ella turned away.

Pity was for the weak.

As they were finally hoarded onto the wooden platform in the middle of the square, Ella flicked a glance at the other men and women that followed her on. They were all in chains and older than her.

Cadeyrn nodded in support. She nodded back, but she wasn't feeling it. Still, she kept her chin high and her eyes cold. If anyone thought about buying her, let them know that she was planning on killing them in their sleep.

Like ye had with the man who'd killed ye father?

Swallowing, Ella tried to hide the shaking of her hands. This time would be different. It had to be…

They were purchased, along with another boy, by a lady in a white, half-sleeved dress. It hung loosely around her body with a wide purple hem along its edge. A red shawl graced her right shoulder, wrapped around her lower back, and came out over her left arm. Her blonde hair was piled high on top of her head and a veil covered her face. What skin Ella could see was pristine and clean.

Looking the woman over, Ella grinned. She'd be easy to escape from. She'd probably never run a day in her life.

"Is there something amusing?" the woman asked, her voice a soft melody.

Ella's grin stretched tight. "Ye are just too beautiful is all."

The woman's smile was kind and radiant. She nodded

at the large man beside her. Ella looked at him in surprise. His skin was so dark it looked as if someone had painted him with the colours of the earth. Ella was about to ask why he'd let someone do that when he stepped forwards and backhanded her across the face.

She stumbled, tripping over her feet, and fell. Her face stung. Cadeyrn growled as he leaped at the man, but he too was knocked down.

Clenching her hands, Ella looked up with a glare. The woman held her gaze.

"Sarcasm," she said ever so softly, "will not be tolerated. Nor will lying. And when you address me, it will be as 'Domina'. Do you understand?"

The man picked her up and backhanded her across the face again. Ella's eyes welled with tears. Her head roared with pain. Gritting her teeth, she sucked up the snot in her throat and spat it at his face. Glowering, he struck her again.

"If you think I will stop him from killing you because I just paid for you," the woman said in that same delightful voice, "you are wrong. I have more coin than I know how to spend."

"Then kill me," Ella growled.

"Ella!" Cadeyrn gasped. She glanced at him, seeing that another man, this one white, had twisted Cadeyrn's arms behind his back. A grimace cut into her friend's face and she knew he was in pain.

"Leave him alone!" She dug her nails into the arm holding her, but even though she drew blood, he did not let her go.

"Break one of his fingers," the woman said flippantly.

Cadeyrn screamed and then so did Ella. She scratched deeper into the arm holding her still, kicked out at the man it was attached to, but he wasn't phased. He didn't move at all.

Cadeyrn fell to his knees, tears running down his cheeks. His arms were still held tightly behind him. Ella's heart broke as she struggled to reach him, but couldn't.

"Break another one."

"No!"

Cadeyrn screamed in pain and so did she. The crowd that had formed around them thickened. Desperately, Ella looked at their faces, silently pleading for one of them to help.

But no one did.

Tears thick with anger, Ella glared at the woman. "I'll kill ye!" she screamed.

"Break another."

Ella's chest heaved as her eyes flew to Cadeyrn. Seeing the raw pain twist his face as the snap of a finger ripped through the tension, brought her to her knees.

"Stop!"

"Stop, what?" the woman murmured.

"Please!"

The woman sighed in disappointment. Ella's heart raced as fear consumed her. Please was what her father was always telling her to say. Please was polite. Please was right. Why wasn't it right?

"Break his ar –"

"Domina!" Ella blurted, fat tears rushing down her cheeks. She prayed that she was right to every god and goddess that hadn't yet abandoned them. "Please, stop, Domina," she begged.

The woman smiled. She waved her hand at the man holding Cadeyrn and he instantly released him. Cadeyrn cradled his hand against his chest, his breaths coming out in shocked gasps.

Ella swallowed hard as she looked at him. Fearing the woman wanted something more, Ella whispered, "Thank ye…Domina."

"Thank *you.*"

She swallowed again. Lowered her head despite the fire in her chest. She would kill this bitch. She would kill everyone in the crowd around them. They would look back on this day and wish they'd done something to help Cadeyrn. Tears of anger rolling down her cheeks, Ella pretended to sniffle. "Thank you, Domina," she said.

The woman watched her in silence. The hair on the back of Ella's neck prickled, but she didn't dare look up. The vengeance in her eyes would be too easily seen.

"You are most welcome," the domina said. Stepping around her, she added, "Continue to learn quickly and you might just survive the year… If the gods are willing."

The gods had abandoned them. Even the blind could see that. Cadeyrn's fingers had been reset the night before, but the fire inside him had died. He couldn't even look at her and Ella was drowning in her guilt. As they walked through the rain, trailing behind the carpentum carrying their domina, Ella tried not to despair.

"Cadeyrn, I'm so sorry," she whispered.

They weren't supposed to be talking, but she couldn't bear the silence of his pain. He hadn't spoken to her since they'd been sold. The only words he'd uttered had been, "Blacksmithing, Domina," when they'd been questioned about their skills.

Hers had been, "Hunting and cooking, Domina."

"Cadeyrn," Ella tried again, eyeing the wagon in front of them. She doubted their domina could hear her over the rattle of the wheels and the patter of the rain, but she didn't want to take any chances. Cadeyrn's screams of pain still echoed in her head and Ella doubted they would ever lessen. She didn't need any more of them keeping her up at night.

"Cade –"

"Shut up," the boy behind her hissed.

Ella turned her head to glare at him. He was older than her, probably around Cadeyrn's age, but he was also a recently bought slave. He didn't hold any position over her, not like the two grown men that had hurt them earlier.

Before she could say anything though, he added, "Tis yer tongue they'll take if they hear ye talking."

She paled. Glancing at Cadeyrn's hand, which he still held cradled against his chest, Ella whispered, "How do ye know?"

He looked at her in confusion. "How do ye not? Have ye heard no stories about Octavia? Where –" He stopped abruptly as the white man turned to look at them.

Ella ducked her head. The rain trickled past her eyes, hiding the fury inside. He had broken Cadeyrn's fingers and his spirit. Ella would kill him. And this time she would not hesitate.

Clenching her jaw, Ella dug her fingers into her thighs. She looked up with a glare. She wanted the man to know she was coming for him. She wanted him to live in fear. But he'd already turned back around, dismissing her anger and pain.

Turning to Cadeyrn, Ella grabbed his good hand in silence. He didn't even look at her as they continued through the rain.

The next morning, they arrived in the military town of Derventio. Their new home was an impressive building, much bigger than the hut Ella had grown up in. Nearing the entrance, the party split. The domina and the dark man went to the front of the house while Ella and the others were led around to the side.

They entered through a short corridor, which led into a large, rectangular garden. It was open to the sky, the edge of its roof held up by wooden pillars every few feet. A small pool surrounded by mosaic tiles sat in the centre of the greenery. Rising out of the water was a life-sized statue of a naked woman.

"Roman!" a well dressed man said as he came striding towards them. He smiled brightly, but the look in his eyes made Ella's stomach curl. It was like he was a wolf and they were unguarded lambs.

Shifting in front of Cadeyrn, Ella watched him warily.

"Dominus," Roman greeted, the use of the title telling them that this newcomer was Flavia's husband.

"What a fine lot Octavia has picked this time," the man beamed. He glanced over at Ella and Cadeyrn before his eyes settled on the other slave boy. Crouching down in front of him, he asked, "What's your name, son?"

"Fial," the boy muttered.

Ella's eyes narrowed as she remembered the Fial that had brought them to Luguwalos.

"And how old are you?" the dominus asked.

"Ten and two."

The man smiled. It wasn't warm though. It was cold and sick and caused the hairs on Ella's neck to rise.

Placing a hand on the boy's shoulder, Roman said, "Domina wants them to help with Aurelia's birthday fe—"

The man waved his hand as he rose, his eyes never leaving Fial's. "But of course. Whatever my wife wants. I can be helped by this one later." His smile widened as he ruffled Fial's hair. Finally looking at Roman, he added, "Make sure he's not too tired to help me tonight."

Roman bowed his head and answered tightly, "Yes, Dominus."

Ushering them along, Roman led them into the culina where they slaved away for hours. They cut up vegetables and meat, kneaded flour until their arms ached, and stirred pots of food they weren't allowed to taste despite the pangs in their stomachs. Then they ferried the food out on pewter plates, only to have to bring them back when they were empty.

So lost in her work, Ella didn't notice Fial's absence part way through. It wasn't until he'd returned that she realised he'd been gone at all.

Eyes narrowing, Ella was about to demand where he'd been and why he felt like he could leave them to do all the washing up when she noticed he was walking oddly. Dry tears crusted his face and his eyes were red and puffy.

She frowned in concern even though her annoyance was still sharp. "Ye okay?" she asked.

He nodded without conviction. A terrible fear began to twist her stomach.

"What happened?" she whispered.

Ignoring her, Fial turned to Cadeyrn. "Dominus wants to see you now."

Cadeyrn paled and Ella knew whatever had happened to Fial was going to happen to her friend. Before she could press for more answers, a wooden spoon landed hard on her rear.

"Get back to work," the chef snapped. She was an old hag with black hair and few teeth. She was hard of hearing and cruel whenever she couldn't make out their words. Ella had only been under her direction for a few hours, but already she'd imagined chopping her up and hiding her in the stew.

When they didn't move fast enough, the hag smacked Fial too. He screamed in such pain, Ella flinched in fear. Whatever the man had done to him had seemingly taken Fial's soul. There was no way a mere human could make such a desolate noise.

Terrified for Cadeyrn, Ella turned to the chef and blurted, "Dominus asked to see me."

The chef studied her with shrewd eyes. Then she glanced at Fial who was now crying, his arms wrapped around himself as if that would stop the pain.

"Ella –" Cadeyrn started, but she cut him off.

"He wanted to see me now," she pressed.

The chef pursed her lips, then turned to Fial. "Stop that!" she roared. "Go clean the pots!"

Muttering about useless help, the woman waddled away.

Cadeyrn grabbed her arm. "Ye can't –"

"Tis my fault ye hand is broken," she hissed as she pulled free. "Tis not fair for ye to suffer twice so soon."

"Ella –"

She shook her head. "Look after Fial," she ordered. "Don't let her hit him again. I'll be back soon."

Turning before she could lose her nerve, Ella hurried out the door. She wasn't sure what she was about to get herself into, but whatever it was would be worth it. She couldn't lose Cadeyrn here. She couldn't lose her last tie to home. They might not have ever spoken a kind word to each other before they'd been taken, but he was all she had. When they'd snapped his fingers, that wasn't all they'd broken.

Twisting her fists in her tunic, Ella made her way to the triclinium where they'd been eating. Octavia and her two daughters were still there, but the man was gone.

"Is the culina cleaned already?" Octavia asked.

The two girls turned towards her. Both pretty and blonde and about her age. Aurelia, the one whose birthday it was, gave her a shy smile. Flavia gave her a leer.

Focusing on her domina, Ella shook her head. "Your husband asked to see me."

The woman's eyes darkened. Flavia jumped to her feet, excitement in her eyes. "Oh, mother, can I do it?" she squealed. "Please, please, please, please, please!"

Ella frowned in confusion. Had what happened to Fial not been their father's doing? How else could Flavia be so happy to experience what had crippled Fial?

Glancing at her daughter, Octavia nodded. Before Ella could understand, Flavia smacked her across the face.

Ella immediately hit her back, fuming with fury.

"Mother!" Flavia cried as she raised a hand to her cheek. Tears glistened her eyes as she turned towards Octavia.

Realisation suddenly dawned, but Ella was too tired to care. Whatever punishment she would receive would be worth it.

"Do I need to break Cadeyrn's other hand?" Octavia asked smoothly. "Or shall I take his eyes this time?"

Ella paled. "Why? Twas I who –"

"Why, *Domina.*"

Wetting her lips, Ella whispered, "Why, Domina."

"Good. Now go see my husband, but you are to start work before dawn. No excuses will be tolerated."

"Mother!" Flavia gasped. "You're just going to let her go after she –"

Looking at her daughter, Octavia shook her head. "Not now, Flavia. You can punish her tomorrow." Smiling, she gestured towards the door. "Perhaps you would like to pick an instrument before bed?"

Grinning, her tears now gone, Flavia skipped out of the dining room.

"You may go now. Marcellus is in his chambers across the atrium."

"Yes…Domina."

The woman smiled as Ella bowed her head and left.

Trying not to think about what horrors awaited her, Ella knocked on the door and entered when he allowed it.

Marcellus was dressed in the same white tunic as before, but his hair was rumpled and unkempt. An odd smell lingered in the air. Sitting up from his sprawled out position on the sofa, his brows furrowed. "What are you doing here?" he asked.

"Cade…" Ella swallowed, her hands twisting. Taking a breath, she raised her chin. "Cadeyrn is helping the chef, so she…she sent me instead."

Marcellus looked her over with leering brown eyes. "How old are you?"

She didn't like the question, but she couldn't say why. "Ten," Ella said slowly.

"Ah, the same age as Aurelia. You're pretty, just like her." He smiled, licking his lips. "She has a mole on her inner leg. Do you have one?"

Ella shook her head.

"Show me."

Frozen, she could only stare.

"Show me and I'll show you mine. Or would you rather go back to the culina?"

Swallowing, Ella dug her nails into her thighs. "What…what did ye do to Fial?"

"We just played a game."

"He was crying. The way he screamed –"

He cut her off with a wave of his hand. "So he's a sore loser."

"But –"

His eyes flashed with irritation. "Hasn't Octavia taught you not to talk back, yet?" He patted the sofa beside him. "Now come here."

Dragging her feet, Ella did as commanded. She was doing this for Cadeyrn, she reminded herself. She was doing this so he wouldn't break. So she wouldn't be alone. Because she wouldn't survive here otherwise.

But she hadn't known there were worse things than being alone…

Chapter Four

Never Give Ye Name
120 Derventio (Papcastle, Earth)

Hidden amongst the trees, Ella picked mindlessly at the grass. Ten and three blades she wrenched up. Ten and three – her lucky number. That was how old she'd been when Marcellus had finally grown tired of her. That was the amount of times he'd been stabbed over a game of dice a year later. The number of days he'd lasted before dying from those wounds.

Ten and three. Ten and three. What beautiful numbers they were.

But not as beautiful as Cadeyrn.

Turning her attention to the riverside, Ella watched him emerge from the trees and pick his way down to the bank. He took off his shoes and tunic, then waded in butt-naked up to his waist. Without a thought to the cold, he dived in. A feeling of longing built up inside Ella's chest.

She wished she was bold enough to join him or at the very least, to tell him how she felt. But he'd been her only light for the last eight years. He'd been her sun and moon and stars. If he didn't return her feelings… If he found it to be too awkward between them afterwards…

But what if he didn't? a little voice whispered. *What if he loved me too…*

Before Ella could respond to the musings of her heart, a high-pitched voice sang out behind her. "Hello!"

Eyes widening, Ella ducked low. She was supposed to be picking mushrooms in time for Felix's feast tonight. He was the son of Hadrian, the Roman Emperor. His arrival had been known for weeks. Everything had to be perfect. If Flavia caught her dallying out here, she would punish Cadeyrn severely.

Staying as still as possible, Ella prayed that Flavia didn't see her. But the gods had long abandoned her and did not hear her plea.

Sneering, Flavia's eyes lit up as she picked her way through the trees. She towered over her, her lips cruel. "What are you doing here?" she asked haughtily.

Smiling tightly, Ella rose with her basket clutched in one hand. The other clenched at her side, digging into her skirts. Her fingers burned startlingly hot through the fabric. "I've been sent to pick penny bun mushrooms," she replied. It was a miracle that she'd managed to say that meekly instead of as the snarl in her head.

Flavia looked pointedly at her empty basket, her lips stretching into a leer. "So where are they?"

"I've only just started."

The smack across her face had been expected. Unlike her mother, Flavia preferred to get her own hands dirty.

Ella's brand on her back had been given by the monster before her. Same with the whip scars along her thighs.

"I've only just started, *Domina,*" Flavia spat. "You will address me properly."

Ella's grip on her basket tightened. Licking the blood off her lip, she straightened her head. Before she could say anything stupid though, Cadeyrn cut in with a surprised, "Ella?"

They both looked over at him. He was dressed now, but his damp clothes hugged him like Ella yearned to. Flavia's eyes heated as they raked down his body. Fighting the urge to claw the woman's eyes out, Ella took a step back.

"What's going on?" he demanded. As a skilled slave and a damn good one, Cadeyrn was given a bit more freedom than her. He glanced at her, causing Flavia's brown eyes to narrow.

A sick feeling twisted in Ella's stomach. That wasn't just any look in Flavia's eyes. That was a look of jealousy.

Please gods, don't let it be so.

But of course, they did not listen.

Fuming, Flavia rounded on Cadeyrn, shoving at his chest. "Have you been fucking this whore behind my back?" she screeched. "Have you slipped your hard cock between her legs like you've been doing to mine?"

His eyes widened as he looked at Ella. Her mouth fell open in horror. Her heart twisted. Out of all the women he could've slept with, why did it have to be her?

"Ella…" he tried to explain as he took a step forward, but she shook her head and took a step back.

"Oh?" Flavia laughed maniacally. "Oh, did you not know? I thought you two shared everything." She turned to her in pleasure. "Shall I enlighten you then?"

"Flavia…" Cadeyrn warned. He grabbed her arm and the contact made Ella's stomach toil in pain.

Sneering, Flavia spun around and slapped him hard across the face. It didn't even turn his head. Cadeyrn had suffered a lot more at the hands of her mother.

"You think just because I let you spill your seed inside me, I'll give you certain liberties?" Flavia snarled at him. "You are a *slave!*" she spat. "I *own* you. You are to n*ever* lay another hand on me unless it is in pleasure. Do you understand?"

Ella watched him clench his teeth. His free hand fisted at his side, but he nodded in understanding. When he went to remove his hand from her arm though, Flavia grabbed it with a cruel smile.

"So pleasure me," she purred. Her eyes held Ella's. Her lips curled into a sneer.

Backpedaling fast, Ella stumbled over her feet. Her hands automatically flew out behind her to brace her fall. They hit the ground a second before her arse did. One hand clenched around a rock. The other dug into the earth.

Cadeyrn shook his head over Flavia's shoulder even as his hand glided across her arm and reached her breast.

"Open your eyes!" Flavia snapped before Ella had even realised she'd closed them. "Take note of what you will *never* have." She hiked up the skirt of her tunic, baring pale thighs that were passionately bruised.

Gritting her teeth, Ella clenched the rock harder. Her heart burned with pain and fury. A fire ignited inside her, but she couldn't let it out. She still recalled Cadeyrn's screams all those years ago as their domina had used him as a means of breaking her.

And today was too special. Felix's arrival meant too much to their domina. If anyone was punished today, Ella knew they would not survive to see tomorrow.

So she gripped her rock and she held onto her anger as she watched like the dutiful slave she was.

But soon, she vowed to herself. Soon, she would burn this place to the ground. And she'd happily sell her soul to do it.

Long after the two had come and gone, Ella sat on the ground, rock in hand, knuckles white. Dried tears cracked her cheeks. Her heart was ripped to pieces, but bound back together with twine.

What she had seen, could never be unseen.

What she had heard, could never be unheard.

Cadeyrn had betrayed her, sleeping with the enemy for who knows how long. And he'd never said a word. Flavia hadn't been the only one who'd thought they'd shared everything…

But aren't ye keeping ye own secret? her heart asked.

Closing her eyes, Ella let out a ragged breath. That was not the same. It's not like she'd slept with the man that had broken Cadeyrn's fingers. Or the one who had whipped his back so fiercely, Cadeyrn had almost died.

Flavia had spent the last eight years making Ella wish for death. She'd beaten her, shared her amongst her male friends, and forced her to commit humiliating act after humiliating act. She was a thousand times worse than her mother. And Cadeyrn…

Cadeyrn had brought her pleasure.

Worse, he'd *enjoyed* it.

On a scream of rage, Ella threw her rock at a tree. How much would these people take from her? How many horrors would they heap on her? How much pain? They had taken her innocence. They had taken Fial, having buried him with Marcellus, forever trapping him with the monster that had caused him the most pain.

They would not take Cadeyrn too.

Climbing to her feet, Ella looked southeast to the lands of the dark fae. For years she'd contemplated venturing in to find the Dark One, but the stories all said he only took one type of payment – the selling of one's soul.

But Ella didn't care anymore. The gods could judge her in the afterlife because she was already living in hell.

Decision made, Ella headed for the hill. She came across a circle of stones, ten and three in number, most of which were taller than her. Wildflowers grew inside it, as did various mushrooms, including penny buns and many she'd never seen before.

Figuring this had to be the place, Ella stepped into the clearing and lifted her chin. "Hello?" she called out, but only the birds answered her. Frowning, she took another step forward. "I'm here to make a deal with the dark fae," she tried again.

Straining her ears, she tried to listen for a mystical voice, but all she heard were the birds and insects. Muttering, Ella shook her head. She was being foolish. There were no fae here. Everyone knew they had left this world long ago.

Placing her basket on the ground, she reached for the closest cluster of penny buns. She's just been about to pick them when a low voice echoed through the meadow.

"Remove them and I will do the same to you."

Jerking to her feet, Ella quickly turned her head. She peered all around her, but did not see the man who had spoken.

"Who's there?" she demanded.

"You come into my home and dare ask who I am?"

She swallowed as a man stepped out from behind one of the stones. He was built to perfection. Broad shoulders. Strong jaw. Lean and fit and beautifully shirtless. His bare chest showed off a web of blue tattoos. But it was his eyes that held her.

His eyes that were old and ancient. That spoke of horrors she could never imagine. That whispered of dangers she would not survive.

Taking a step back, Ella wetted her lips. "Are…are ye the fae?"

He studied her with his dark eyes. They were as black as his hair, bottomless voids of chaos that led straight to the Otherworld. It was as if he was peering into her soul, weighing her worth and finding it too light to give a damn.

Digging her fingers into her thighs, Ella raised her chin. He smiled lazily, but it was far too feral to be nice.

"Want do you want?" he asked as he began to circle her, his eyes detailing every inch of her form. Her skin flushed under the heat of his gaze. When he stopped at her back and stepped close, his breath tickled her cheek. His chest grazed her back. If she turned to look at him, his lips would touch her skin. If she tilted her head, she would taste him. Swallowing hard, Ella fought the urge to do either of those things. She was here for a reason and it wasn't to get taken by a fae – regardless of what her body suddenly craved.

"I want…"

She sucked in a breath as he stepped closer. His hands started on her hips and trailed up. She could feel him everywhere now. Her body was on fire, sensitive to every little touch of his fingers.

"Stop that," she rasped. But even to her, it sounded more like a plea for him to continue.

"Just tell me what you want," he whispered in her ear. His tongue caressed her lobe before he sucked it in between his teeth.

Ella jerked on a wave of bliss. Dear gods. What she wanted and what she *wanted* right now were entirely different things.

Her fingers dug into her thighs as she tried to think past the desire pooling between her legs.

"I want…"

His lips slid down her neck and to her shoulder, pushing aside the fabric of her tunic. Ella closed her eyes, her breath shaky and unsure.

In all of her years, she had never known pleasure by the touch of a man. They had always given her pain. Wary of the new sensations, Ella jerked away from his touch.

The fae were known for their trickery, she told herself as she crossed her arms. He was just trying to distract her, to get her to ask for a favour that was far easier for him to give.

Spinning around to face him, Ella said, "I want them to die."

He looked at her in amusement, no ounce of lust in his dark eyes. It was unnerving…and oddly hurtful.

"Who?" he asked calmly.

She hesitated, still stuck on the feel of his lips.

Shaking her head, she said, "Flavia, Octavia, all of them." She dug her nails into her arms as her hatred once again consumed her. The fog in her brain slowly started to clear.

He studied her in silence before asking, "Why now?"

"What?"

"You've been a slave for eight years. Why kill them now?"

"How do ye –" She stopped. It didn't matter how he knew. All that mattered was that he could free her and Cadeyrn.

"Is it because of him?" he murmured. Something flashed across his eyes too fast for Ella to identify.

"Who?" But she knew who. Cadeyrn was the only male that mattered to her.

"The man you watched in the river." He took a step closer, his eyes holding hers in a grip she could not break. "The man you watched swim naked under the morning sun while you slipped a hand beneath your –"

"I did not!" she protested, her cheeks flushing a deep crimson.

He smiled lazily and slow. Taking another step, he closed the distance between them. Picking up a strand of her hair, he twirled it around a finger. Tugging her close, he whispered in her ear. "But you wanted to."

Ella shook her head, but she couldn't find her voice to properly deny it. He had taken all of her breath away, drew it into himself as if it was his right.

"Oh, yes," he murmured as he looked into her eyes. "You watched the water running through his hair, wishing it were your hands." He glided his fingers through her fiery red hair, cupping the back of her head. His eyes dipped to her neck. "You watched the droplets form on his skin, wishing they were your lips." She quivered as his mouth grazed her sensitive flesh. "And you watched the water part for his body, wishing it were your thighs." He stepped between her legs, his hands dropping to her ass. Hauling her against him, he smiled.

"What…what are ye doing?" Ella quivered, her breaths coming quick and fast.

"It has been a long time since I've had the company of another…" He trailed off, staring at her mouth. "And a favour asked requires a favour paid."

She wet her lips. "And is a favour of the flesh what ye are after?"

He smiled. "No. As beautiful as you are, I require something else."

"What?"

"Your name."

She blinked. "That's it?"

"That's it."

"But that can't be –"

"Just your name," he whispered in her ear, "and I will help you kill the ones you call Domina."

She no longer cared that the deal seemed too good to be true. Filled with desire, Ella nodded. "Ell-"

"No. Your full name," he cut in, straightening his head to look at her.

Her brows furrowed in confusion. She didn't understand what difference it made, but then, what did it matter? If it led to Flavia's death, then she would gladly give whatever name he wanted. "Fionnghula," she said.

His lips curled into a true smile. For a moment, she thought she saw triumph flash across his eyes, but it was gone so quickly, she couldn't be sure.

"Fionnghula," he said and it was as if he was licking

honey off her skin. His eyes crinkled. Their dark depths drew her in like a moth to the flame. "Fionnghula, my sweet," he drawled as he ran his hands up her waist, "I accept your deal."

Chapter Five

Run Baby Run

So what's ye name?" Ella demanded, stepping back so she could think clearly. There was something about the fae that was muddling her thoughts and making it hard to concentrate. Never before had she wanted to know a man. Even with Cadeyrn, she had to stop herself from shying away from his touch.

But with the fae…

Looking into his eyes, Ella wanted to explore every inch of his skin. She shook her head. He had to be bewitching her.

With a slow smile, the Dark One leaned against one of the large stones. He glanced down her body. Everywhere his gaze lingered, Ella's skin tingled with desire. Her neck. Her breasts. Her –

"Well?" she demanded, her face flushed.

His gaze travelled back up to meet her own. "You can call me Daman."

"Well, Daman." She cleared her throat. Unable to help herself, she peaked at his naked chest. Even if he'd been a mere human, his strength and power radiated with something more. "What do the tattoos mean?" she asked as her eyes followed a blue path down the centre of his torso. She wet her lips as it disappeared beneath his trousers. *Did it go all the way?*

"Yes."

Startled, Ella looked up. She was horrified that she'd actually asked that aloud. Shaking her head, she snapped, "What are ye doing to me?"

"What do you mean?"

"Ye are making me…" Waving her hand, she searched for the words.

"Yes?" he murmured. A jolt of desire ran through her. His voice had deepened. His gaze had focused, darkened.

Nervous, she wet her lips again. He took a step closer, his eyes never leaving hers.

"What do I make you feel, Fionnghula?" The way he'd whispered her name caused her to shiver.

She took a step back like a coward. And another. And another. Gripping her basket until her knuckles turned white, she asked, "So when will ye do it?"

"Soon," he murmured and Ella had the suspicious feeling that he wasn't talking about the same thing she was.

Swallowing, she mumbled, "I…I have to go."

"Not yet." He stepped in front of her. His eyes dipped to her lips. Her breasts. Trailing a finger across her cheek, he slipped his hand through her hair and tilted her head back.

Ella's breath hitched as she stood frozen in his gaze.

"I doona –"

He moved too fast, stealing her protest. His lips claimed hers. His tongue swept inside and suddenly, her protest was forgotten entirely.

He walked her backwards. He angled her head so he could deepen the kiss, so he could brand her with his mark of possession. His hands trailed down her back to her ass. Squeezed before going lower. They gripped the fabric of her skirts and pulled them up. He stepped closer, one of his thighs pushing between her legs. She felt the cool wind a second before the heat of his touch.

Gasping, Ella tried to back away only to find there was nowhere to go. A tree hit her back. He stepped closer, moving his hands up her body until he claimed her breasts.

His mouth devoured her. His tongue marked her and his breath filled her lungs. She tried to turn her head, but then his lips were on her neck and she was crying out in desperation. But not in a desperation to escape.

No, she wanted this. Craved it, even though she had always hoped her first real time would be with a green eyed lad that had once called her mother a Roman whore.

"Daman…" She moaned, leaning her head to the side. She basked in the feel of his lips as he trailed them down to her shoulder.

Closing her eyes, Ella had just weaved her fingers through his hair when Daman suddenly stepped back. Her lips felt swollen in the wind. Her eyes half lidded, she looked at him in confusion.

"Now you can go," he said. "Run north and don't stop until you hit the road."

She blinked. There wasn't an ounce of lust in his eyes. Just inhuman indifference that hurt more than she cared to admit. "W– What?"

"Go!" he roared loud enough to shake the trees.

Terrified, Ella stumbled back. She tripped over her feet, cut her hand on a rock. As Daman began to change shape in front of her, Ella's eyes grew wide. Throwing the rock at the shifting blob, she jumped to her feet and ran.

A demonic sound howled behind her. Blood pounded in her ears. Scrambling down the hill, Ella was harshly reminded of her escape attempt with Cadeyrn.

A fierce growl had her picking up speed. She tripped. Her knees hit the ground and she skidded, scraping them both. Turning onto her back, Ella backpedaled quickly, her eyes searching the foliage for whatever beast chased her.

The idiocy of her plan slammed home. The fae were a race not to be messed with. They kidnapped children and ate them. And Daman was the worst; he was so evil, he'd been left behind by the others when they 'd abandoned this world. Everyone knew the tales. Everyone knew to stay well away from his home.

Heart pounding, Ella tracked the shape darting through the trees. It was massive and black and looked like death. It was going so fast. There was no way she'd even be able to react before he was on her.

"Run!"

Eyes widening, Ella scrambled to her feet. That word had been more like a growl. It hadn't been human. It had been feral, animalistic.

He was going to play with her.

But what could she do but run?

Dashing through the trees, Ella lost track of all sense of direction. She just ran in the opposite direction of the growls and snapping teeth. Every so often she tripped over her feet, but he never advanced. She never got a good look at Daman in his animal form.

Exploding from the trees, Ella stumbled into the road. She didn't see the advancing party until it was too late. A horse reared, its reins pulled hard by its rider. The sight of hooves caused her to trip, but all of Ella's concern was taken up by the fae behind her.

She twisted on the ground, eyes wide, mouth agape. She searched the trees, certain he would not stop. Roman soldiers had nothing on the Dark One. Daman would rip them to shreds before they could even draw their swords. It was why they had always given his home a wide berth despite his chaos to their rule.

"Who are –"

"Behind ye!" Ella screamed as she pointed. A giant wolf jumped from the trees and took the man right off his horse. Blood spurted into the air. The other half dozen soldiers cried out as they wrestled their steeds under control. A sword sang free. An arrow whistled and the wolf howled in pain.

Ella sucked in a breath, her pulse jolting in both fear for his safety and relief that he could be stopped. She didn't understand her emotional investment in the fae, but there was no denying the tight clench in her chest.

With a wild yelp, the wolf lunged across the road. He passed her, his eyes holding no trace of pain despite the arrow sticking out of his hind. If anything, it looked like he was smiling. As another arrow pierced him though, that smile turned into annoyance.

Ella's mouth dropped open, so confused she couldn't

move. A man slammed her to the ground and rolled her to safety. But she'd never been in any danger.

She knew that now. Watching Daman disappear into the trees, she knew with absolute certainty that he would never hurt her.

So why all the bloody theatrics? Why scare the living shite out of her? Before she could scream at him, a man yelled out from behind her.

"Where did it go?"

Eyes widening, she looked over her shoulder. But all she could see was a smooth cut jaw and the most beautiful eyes in the world. They were a stunning blue, as clear as the sea on a summer day, as bright as the sky at midday.

"Are you hurt?" the man asked and his voice was the most beautiful melody. Deep and baritone and capable of making her toes curl.

Blinking, Ella stared in awe. Before she could reply, the newcomer shouted again, "The wolf! Where did it go?"

Surprised, Ella squirmed beneath the man that had tackled her. She knew that voice. That was –

Her jaw dropped. *Daman!*

"It went into the woods!" one of the soldiers shouted.

Cursing, Daman growled, "It's long gone then. That's its territory and only a fool will hunt such a beast in its home."

Looking at Ella and the man still on top of her, Daman's eyes narrowed. "Did the lass get bitten?"

"I don't think she's hurt," the man answered.

"Then why are ye still on top of her?"

Clearing his throat, the man climbed to his feet. He held out a hand and Ella took it to stand. She faced

Daman, her eyes expressing her many questions. Like how was he suddenly dressed in a kilt? How had he appeared behind them so quickly when she'd just watched him disappear in front of her?

Catching her eye, Daman smiled lazily. "I can see why ye stayed on top of her for so long," he murmured. "She is a beauty."

Ella blushed, remembering the taste of his lips all too easily. Not even a few minutes ago, he'd had his hands on her arse and a thigh between her –

"Me name's Daman," the fae said, holding out his hand to the man in front of her.

"Felix," the soldier said, grasping it.

Her eyes widened. She looked around her, suddenly taking in the many well-dressed guards and well-groomed horses. Dear gods, this was Felix. *The* Felix. Octavia's Felix. Hadrian's Felix. The successor to the bloody Roman Empire Felix.

And Daman…

Daman had chased her straight into his path.

Chapter Six

What Could Be

He was a good man," Felix said solemnly. He stood over the body of his fallen comrade. The soldier's head had been ripped half off his shoulders and his eyes now stared lifelessly at his arse. "We shall tell his wife that he died bravely in battle," the emperor's son added.

He didn't have the chance to fight at all, Ella thought as she glanced at Daman. The kill had been too quick.

She sucked in a small breath when the fae caught her eye. He stared at her hotly, his gaze flicking to her chest. Ella glanced down and scrambled to fix her tunic. There wasn't much that could be done though. Her tumble earlier had ripped a hole right between her breasts.

Pulse thundering, Ella took a small step back from all

the men. In her experience, it didn't take much to tempt them and she was easily identified as a slave. Octavia was well known to be…generous with the sharing of her live property.

When Felix suddenly turned towards her, Ella couldn't help but flinch. It was bad form to take a slave without one of their dominuses' permission, but he was the son of the emperor. Nothing would be denied him.

Shockingly though, when his eyes dipped to the rip in her clothes held tightly together by white knuckled hands, he didn't leer with lust. He frowned with concern.

"Are you hurt?" he asked and he genuinely seemed to mean it. Ella didn't think for a moment that he was merely trying to get a better look at her naked breasts.

Flicking a glance at the other men, her eyes lingered for half a beat on Daman's. His jaw was clenched tight. His eyes were hard. It was as if he was forcing himself from doing something he desperately wanted to do.

Hurriedly, Ella looked back at Felix.

"It is okay," he murmured. "My men will not hurt you." Undoing the clasp at his shoulder, he pulled his purple paludamentum cloak free and handed it to her. After a moment's hesitation, Ella took it. One side of the rip fell free as she did so, but Felix never broke her gaze. Not even for a quick peek.

Offering a small smile in thanks, Ella clutched the cloak to her chest.

"It would be easiest if you put it on," he grinned.

She knew that. She just didn't know how to wear it since Octavia had never given them any kind of cloak even in the dead of winter.

Seeing her confusion, Felix's eyes softened. "May I?" he asked as he reached for the paludamentum.

Looking deep into his eyes, Ella realised she could trust him. He might be the heir to a brutal empire, but the man himself was kind. Nodding, she released the cloak to him and stood patiently as he wrapped it around her properly.

Looking over her shoulder, Ella sought out Daman again. Desire flooded her under the intensity of his gaze. Unlike Felix, he stared right at her breasts. They were covered now, but even still they felt as if they were not. Lips parting, Ella remembered the touch of his hands, the feel of his kiss…

Smirking, the fae raised a hand to his jaw and rubbed a thumb across his lower lip.

Dear gods, she wanted him.

Blinking rapidly, Ella focused back on Felix. He was asking her something, his head still lowered as he finished straightening the paludamentum.

"Um… Nay, I have no injuries."

"You're covered in cuts and bruises," he replied as he looked up and moved his hand to the side of her face. As soon as she flinched though, he stopped with a frown. Understanding softened his gaze and he took a step back to give her space.

Ella smiled in thanks even though her struggle to breathe wasn't due to the proximity of a man this time. It was because she knew that Daman still looked at her as if he yearned to ravage her senseless.

"Thank ye," she said with a small bow.

"You are most welcome." His smile was radiant and pure. Two dimples flashed at the corners of his lips.

Turning back around, he addressed his men about burying their comrade. As four of them moved the body off the side of the road, the last one rode off on his horse towards Derventio, presumably to find tools to do the job.

"Have you been hunting this beast for long?" Felix asked Daman.

The fae scowled in frustration. "Too long, aye. Its mother was terrorising the lands around Ravenglass for months before I killed her. But I did not know she had a wee pup. Been chasing this bastard all over the fells." He was so convincing in his lie that even Ella believed him.

"It's been terrorising Ravenglass, but its den is there?" Felix asked, nodding at the trees on the other side of the road.

Daman's scowl deepened. "Tis smart, this beast. The black dogs know better than to eat where they shite. Me and me kind" – he thumped his chest with pride – "have been hunting these hounds for generations. We know all their tricks, aye. Yet, every year they get smarter and smarter" – he tapped his temple, his eyes wary – "giving us a good run along these fells."

"Your kind?" Felix asked.

Daman smiled. "No offense to ye attempt to conquer us, but I am still a Brigante. We know these lands like ye never will."

Shocking her again, Felix didn't take any offense. He nodded in understanding. "The Roman Empire thanks you for your service. When we get to Derventio, I will send men out to aid you."

Daman shook his head. "They will only get killed. Night is the black dog's terrain. Only ever hunt them during the day if ye want to go home to yer wife after."

"Your wisdom is most appreciated."

Daman grinned slyly. "Enough to give me a ride into town? I can ride that wee steed there. Save ye from needing someone to lead it."

"But of course. I would have insisted as I'd like to learn more about these beasts."

"Over a meal, perhaps?" Daman asked and Felix nodded.

Struggling to hide her awe, Ella looked down at her feet. Within minutes, Daman had implemented himself into Felix's party. Octavia's was the richest family on this island. It would take the son of the emperor himself to bend her to his will.

Giddy with excitement at the prospect of Octavia and Flavia dying so soon, Ella missed what Felix had said.

"Felix, I must –" one of the guards began.

"It's fine, Julius," he cut in with a wave of his hand. "She means me no harm." His eyes danced as he looked at her. "Isn't that right?"

Ella shook her head. She might not know what they were talking about, but there was only one way to answer such a question. "Nay. I mean, aye. Nay, wait – I –" She took a deep breath. "I mean ye no harm."

His eyes told her he was laughing at her now, but it wasn't in a cruel way. It was soft and sweet and Ella couldn't help but smile at him.

"Good," he murmured. "Then we shall ride."

He gestured her towards his horse, a massive roan with a white line running from its mane to its nose. Nervously, Ella approached. It pawed at the ground and she was instantly reminded of her close call with a set of hooves not too long ago.

"Aithon is a gentle soul," he murmured. "He will not harm you."

With a firm nod, Ella raised her chin. Felix helped her up and then swung up behind her. When he wrapped his arms around her waist to grab the reins, she tried not to tense. As beautiful and kind as Felix was, she still didn't like his touch.

Still, what could she do? Ask to ride with Daman? A man she wasn't supposed to know?

Glancing over at him, Ella's mouth watered. The fae's muscles flexed as he pulled himself up onto a solid black horse. He looked like one of Octavia's statues, so perfect was his body. Her fingers itched to trail along his back, wrap around his waist, and dip beneath his kilt.

As if hearing her thoughts, Daman looked at her sharply. His eyes lingered on her lips. His nostrils flared and a corner of his mouth curled.

"So what were you doing out here all by yourself?" Felix asked, dragging her attention away from Daman.

With a groan, Ella sagged forward. Octavia was going to kill her. She'd dropped her bloody basket when Daman had started to chase her. No wait... That wasn't right. She'd dropped it when he'd kissed her. Or was it...

Cursing, she knew it didn't matter when she'd dropped it. The effect was the same. She didn't have the penny bun mushrooms she'd been sent out to gather. Daman's plan better work quickly because Ella was as good as dead once they got back to Derventio.

"I take it your task was interrupted by the black dog?" Felix pressed.

"Aye." Ella scowled, shooting a glare at Daman.

"Then I will let your dominus know that it could not have been helped. No one should be punished for having run into such a deadly beast."

"Octavia –"

"Ah! Octavia is good friends with my father. A harsh woman, but fair. Fear naught. I will be your champion."

"Ye already have been," Ella replied, tugging on the

cloak he had placed on her shoulders. "And I am most thankful to ye."

"Thankful enough to tell me your name?" he teased.

Taken by surprise, Ella twisted her head to look at him. His blue eyes peered into hers. His lips were so close now, she could almost feel them on hers already. Caressing and tender. He would not ravage her like Daman had. He'd take his time, build her up slowly.

Clearing her throat, Ella asked, "What do ye want me name for?"

"Well, you know mine. It's only fair, I would think." His eyes crinkling, he added, "Although I do have other motives, I must admit. I would like to know to whom I am indebted."

"Indebted?" she asked incredulously.

"Oh, yes." He nodded, his face so serious she couldn't help but laugh. He smiled in response. "Had it not been for you, I would have had a boring ride these last few miles."

"But surely that is not enough to make the emperor's son feel indebted to a slave?"

"Normally, no," he admitted. "But then, there's no one as beautiful as you."

Blushing, Ella didn't know what to say to that. Cruel and crude jokes, she could handle. But compliments? Kindness? *Actual flirting*?

The only kindness she had received was from Cadeyrn and this man was not him. He didn't have that tainted edge to him. He didn't have their history. Felix was a powerful man, but he had nothing on her friend.

"Well?" Felix pressed gently.

She looked at Daman, but he was staring straight ahead. Frustrated at not knowing what she was supposed to do, Ella answered the bloody question.

"Ella," she said a bit tightly. That had once been a name she'd only given to friends, but now it was all she went by. Her dominas and the other Romans didn't like her real name. It was too unpronounceable, they'd said.

Her eyes flicked back to Daman. But he'd said it. And he'd said it as if it was a sin.

"It's a lovely name," Felix murmured.

"Tell me parents. I had no say in it."

He laughed at that. It was rich and pure. Catching his good humour, Ella grinned and sat up a bit straighter.

They talked all the way to twon. It was surprisingly easy too. Ella had kept to herself these last eight years, but there was something about Felix that made her tongue loose. He did not judge. He did not dismiss her simply because of her station. For the first time in a long time, she felt like she mattered.

When they reached the estate, Octavia and her two daughters came out to greet them. Her domina was less than pleased, but she stayed polite in front of Felix. Fearing worse retribution if she hung around, Ella quietly slipped away during the introductions.

She made her way to the side door and into the culina. The chef threw a pan at her for not bringing back any mushrooms, but Ella had expected it and managed to dodge.

Jumping straight into her work, she wondered how long it would be until she was free. She had glimpsed life as someone other than a slave and by the gods, did she want it.

Chapter Seven

happily Ever... La di da

Gritting her teeth, Ella pounded on the dough a lot harder than was necessary. Every time she hit it, she imagined Cadeyrn and Flavia. Him with his hands on her. Him with his cock inside her. Him with pleasure written all over his face.

Scowling, Ella slammed the dough down onto the table. Gods, she wished she hadn't spied on him this morning. That might have led her to Daman and then to Felix, but she'd trade even her potential freedom to take back all she'd seen and heard.

Cadeyrn. She growled. *With Flavia.* She was going to be sick.

"Ella?"

Her head jerked up at the tentative sound of her name.

Her heart both blossomed and deflated at the sight of Cadeyrn standing in front of her.

"Go away," she snapped. "Can ye not see I'm busy?"

"I want to explain."

"I doona want to hear it."

"But ye don't understand."

"Oh, I understand all right," she growled as she slapped the dough on the table. "I understand ye –

"Flavia said she would stop singling ye out," he hissed.

Ella stopped kneading. Turning to face him fully, she snorted. "And ye believed her?"

"Aye. Nay. Maybe. I doona know…" Cadeyrn dragged a hand through his hair, ruffling his ginger curls. "But I had to try. Ye protected me from Marcellus. I just wanted to do the same."

Looking into his pained green eyes, Ella found her anger fading. Turning back to her kneading, she sighed, "Ye better start chopping those vegetables before Chef sees ye just standing there."

Smiling in relief, he started to work alongside her. She glanced at him every so often. There were so many things she wanted to ask him. So many more things she wanted to tell him. But her heart was still sore despite her decision to forgive him.

She had loved him for nearly eight years. Crushed on him for six. She'd imagined a future with him, had used that fantasy to get through her time with Marcellus and the other more severe punishments. Cadeyrn had been her everything, but what was she to him?

He obviously cared for her. The two of them were so close, Octavia used them to punish each other. That was the only thing that had kept them in line. The only thing that had kept them alive. For surely, Ella would have pushed her boundaries until she was killed otherwise.

Done kneading, Ella placed the dough to the side so it could rise overnight. Felix's feast had already started and they were working on tomorrow's breakfast. Soon, they would have to collect the dirty plates and wash them before retiring for bed.

"How did he like it?" Ella asked as she and Cadeyrn began cleaning the culina.

Octavia had had him working on a present for Felix. It was a beautiful knife, intricately carved with symbols for protection. Ella wasn't supposed to have seen it, but Cadeyrn had sneaked it away for her to view the other day. It was by far his best work.

"I doona know. I was not there for the giving, but Octavia has not sent Roman for me. I take it that means he liked it well enough."

"I'm sure he loved it," Ella assured him. "He seems like a kind man."

"Oh, and how would ye know? He seemed smitten with ye when we were serving the table, but ye two didn't pass a word."

Ella grinned. "Not there, aye."

"What?" he exclaimed.

Turning, the Chef chucked a wooden spoon at him. Her hearing might have mostly gone, but her aim was as solid as always.

"Ye better have that bread worked by the time I'm back!" she shouted at the top of her lungs. Grumbling about good-for-nothing helpers, she then wiped her hands on her apron and waddled outside.

He waited until he was certain she wasn't coming back. Then lowering his voice, he demanded, "Tell me everything."

Delighted to have their friendship feeling like it used to, Ella happily obliged. After she'd finished, Cadeyrn shook his head.

"Trading with the fae is dangerous, Ella. Ye should not have done it." Scowling, he muttered, "And ye definitely shouldn't have let him –" He stopped suddenly, his nostrils flaring. After a quick look to make sure Chef wasn't about to walk through the door, he threw down his rag and turned to face Ella fully. "Did ye like it?" he demanded.

"What?"

"His lips on ye. His tongue down ye throat. His hands on ye arse."

Shocked, Ella could only stare. A giddy hope started to build in her chest. Cadeyrn was jealous. The way he was looking at her now was the same way she glanced at him when she'd thought no one was looking.

"Well?"

"Aye," Ella breathed, delighting in the tight clenching of his jaw. She wanted to lean up on her toes and kiss his tic. She wanted to trail her hands down his shoulders and feel the erratic pulse in his chest.

"Aye?" he growled, lowering his head along with his voice. "*Aye*?"

"Aye."

She had barely gotten out the word when his mouth descended. His lips were demanding in what he wanted and confident that he would get it. His tongue ran across her bottom lip before he sucked it into his mouth. She gasped and he took quick advantage.

Sliding his tongue inside, Cadeyrn claimed every inch of her soul. And gods was it beautiful. It was everything she'd imagined and more.

Running her hands through his hair, Ella stepped closer. He touched her breasts. One hand trailed around to her arse. Hauling her against him, Cadeyrn rubbed her nipple between two fingers and his cock between her legs. Moaning, Ella sagged against him.

But he'd chosen just that moment to take a step back.

Stumbling forward, Ella caught herself on the table. Looking up, she was delighted to see his breaths coming in quick and fast. There wasn't any cold indifference like with Daman. There was a matching heat to her fire. A desire to kiss her all over again.

Instead, Cadeyrn crossed his arms and demanded, "Was he as good as that?"

Nay…and aye. Aye and nay. Ella didn't know what to say.

Taking her silence as her being too overwhelmed to think, Cadeyrn smiled smugly. He leaned forwards and kissed her lips again, this time quickly and gently.

"Meet me in the woods at midnight," he whispered just as Chef reentered the culina with a basket full of vegetables.

Quickly focusing back on her tasks, Ella struggled to get her breathing under control. Her thoughts, however, took a lot longer to put to order.

As Cadeyrn left to collect the dirty dishes from the feast outside, Ella touched her lips and smiled.

Finally.

Finally, life was looking up. Daman had agreed to kill Octavia and Flavia. Felix liked her, maybe even enough to grant her her freedom after their deaths. And Cadeyrn… Cadeyrn loved her just as much as she did him. Finally, everything was falling into place.

And finally, for the first time in years, it seemed as if the gods had returned to her side.

If only she'd known that goddess was Delentia, the Incarnation of Madness, Ella wouldn't have celebrated yet.

Chapter Eight

The Fire Inside

Midnight couldn't come fast enough. Ella sat on the purple and gold couch in Felix's chambers. He'd summoned her after the feast to enquire about her health. But although she was enjoying her talk with him, there wasn't any of the raw passion she experienced with Daman nor the years of history she shared with Cadeyrn. Felix might be kind and sweet and everything a lady should dream of, but Ella wasn't a lady. She'd never been a lady, and she never would be. That opportunity had been stolen from her from the moment she'd been taken by the Selgovae.

Taking her short responses and lack of attention to mean she was tired, Felix quickly apologised for keeping her. He offered her his hand to help her rise, then walked her back to the atrium where all the slaves slept. Tiptoeing past the slumbering bodies, Ella smiled politely at Felix. She thanked him for his concern and then waited for him to leave. As soon as he'd disappeared around the corner, she sneaked outside and made her way to the woods.

The moonlight was bright enough to guide her way with ease. Slipping into the cover of the trees, Ella found a spot on a log and waited.

Not even a minute had passed before she heard someone moving through the brush in front of her. Excitement warred with trepidation. Unable to see who it was though, Ella stayed as still as possible, hoping and praying that it was who she thought it was.

"My sweet Fionnghula waits for me in the moonlight," a husky voice murmured in her ear.

She jumped in surprise. She'd almost screamed out of instinct, but Daman's hand had covered her mouth and now it played with her lips as the pulse beat erratically at her neck.

His thumb stroked her lower lip once, twice as he took her earlobe in between his teeth.

"What are ye…" She swallowed her protest when he kissed her neck. She wanted to tell him to stop, that she was waiting for Cadeyrn, but she couldn't find the strength.

"You are mine now, Fionnghula. I can do with you what I please."

She shivered, but it wasn't out of fear. It should have been. For any rational person, it would have been. But he'd said it so huskily, so possessively and his hands were working erotic magic alongside his tongue…

Moaning, Ella arched her back as he cupped her

breasts. Her head fell to the side to give him better access to her neck.

"That's it," Daman murmured as he rubbed his thumbs across both of her nipples. "Give yourself to me."

One hand slipped down her stomach, leaving a trail of sensation across her belly, her thighs. As he pulled her tunic up her leg, Ella turned her head, searching for his lips.

Just before he'd touched her intimately though, Ella gasped and scurried away. "Cadeyrn!"

She was waiting for Cadeyrn.

"Ah, yes," Daman murmured as he watched her with unnaturally dark eyes. "Your true love."

Leaping gracefully over the log, he joined her on the other side of it. Trailing two fingers down her cheek, he stepped close and kissed her again despite her weak protests.

Her heart begged her to stop him, but her body was dying for him to continue. Daman stroked her fire unlike any other, even Cadeyrn. The skill of his hands, the finesse of his lips…

She wanted more and she wasn't strong enough to resist.

Sagging against him, Ella pulled at his kilt. Perhaps if she slated her thirst quickly, she would finally be able to think sensibly around him.

But his hands grabbed hers, stilling them as he stepped back. "Not yet."

"What?"

He released her, but didn't move to give her any space. The heat of his body still wrapped around her, making her pulse everywhere with need.

"There are things you need to know before Samhain

tomorrow."

She blinked. Then she blinked again as irritation came over her. Taking a step back, Ella crossed her arms. "Ye kind does like to play with us, aye? Tell me, do ye really eat children too as the tales say?"

"If they're annoying and plump enough." He'd said it so bluntly, Ella wasn't sure if he'd been joking or not.

"And are ye planning on eating me after all this?"

"You are not a child." He took a step closer. His eyes dipped to her breasts before coming back up to meet her gaze. "You are a queen," he said.

She snorted. "I am but a slave. I toil all day, every day, grinding me fingers until they're bleeding stubs I can no longer feel." She held up her hands to show him. He didn't even look.

"You are a queen," he simply repeated.

Ella shook her head. Then her eyes widened in sudden understanding. "Ye mean I am to marry Felix? Is that why ye chased me into his path this morning?"

Daman scowled, a darkness hardening his eyes. "I did not put you in his path so you could become a trinket on his arm. I introduced you so you could take revenge on your brothers' killer."

Ella shook her head. She might not have known Felix for long, but she could not match such an atrocity to his kind demeanor.

"What are ye talking about?" she demanded

"Before Felix came here, he rode north of Luguwalos. The Selgovae and Novantae are revolting. He helped stop the newest attack and in doing so, he killed three of your brothers. The man I'd ripped from his horse had killed the other." His voice rang with honesty. "Only one of your adopted family remains now, Ella."

"'Tis cannot be true."

"Facts are not changed by your personal feelings." He was getting irritated, but she didn't care. He'd just told her her family was dead.

"Who… Who's alive?" she rasped.

"The youngest."

"Ailill…" He'd just started walking when she'd been taken. To be all alone at his age… Her heart broke for him. And her anger burned.

"Tell me how to kill him," she demanded.

Daman smiled. "Tomorrow during Samhain when our worlds are the closest, you will lay claim to the fire as is your birthright."

"Lay claim to the…" She trailed off in confusion.

"You are a powerful fire elementalist, Fionnghulla. I could sense your magic as soon as you stepped into my home. No human can cross inside the stones." He stepped closer and threaded his fingers through her hair. Grabbing a fistful of her bright red curls, he tilted her head back to look into her soul.

"You are like me – both better and stronger than the humans that plague this earth. And tomorrow, you will free this place of their stench."

She might not have understood everything he'd said, but she believed him. She'd known her entire life that she was different. There was a fire inside her that had never been extinguished. It burned with a need for release, a need to feed.

As a terrible rage clawed at her heart, Ella clenched her fists. For eight years she'd suffered. She'd been beaten and starved and humiliated to no end. Her family had been slaughtered, her father right in front of her. The Romans had taken everything from her and she wanted them dead more than she wanted her freedom.

"That's it," Daman purred. "Hold on to that fire. Feed it with your thirst for vengeance."

Eyes blazing with the power of her ancestors, Ella growled, "I want them all to burn."

"And so they shall."

Crushing her mouth with his, he thrust his tongue inside. As he claimed every inch of her soul, Ella felt the desire rising inside her. She wanted this even though she also wanted Cadeyrn.

But he hadn't come, a little voice whispered. Cadeyrn had stood her up. He might be sliding between Flavia's legs this very instant.

Nostrils flaring, Ella yanked at Daman's kilt. It fell to the ground in a pile of no regrets. She'd just skimmed her fingers across his cock when a pained voice called out from the darkness.

"Ella?"

Freezing, her heart stuttered to a stop. Blood drained from her cheeks as she pushed Daman away and swirled around. Cadeyrn stood staring at her, a broken heart written all over his face.

"I –" She took a step towards him, but Daman grabbed her wrist and yanked her back.

He wrapped his arms around her, caging her against his chest. "You choose him," he growled, "and you will always have to compete with Flavia." He reached in from behind her and tucked a strand of hair behind her ear. Leaning down to whisper, he added, "And Aurelia."

Ella jerked as if she'd been slapped. She didn't want to believe it, but Cadeyrn's guilty face told her it was true.

"Did Aurelia promise ye something too?" she rasped.

Aurelia had never gone out of her way to punish either

of them, but why else would Cadeyrn sleep with her?

"No," Daman answered when it was clear Cadeyrn would not. "He is but a slave and she is his domina. He knows satisfying her will give him certain privileges."

"That's not –" Cadeyrn stopped, but Ella knew what he'd been about to say. She could read it all over his face.

"Ye love her?" she choked.

He took a step forward, one arm reaching out. "Not like ye," he rasped with a shake of his head.

"But she can give him what you cannot," Daman said. "Surely, you cannot be mad at him for that."

Nay.

Nay, Ella would forgive him anything and Cadeyrn knew it. Daman was right. To choose her friend, as much as she loved him, was to choose a life of misery. A life as a slave. He could offer her nothing.

But how could she give him up? Cadeyrn was her everything. What was the point of freedom if she had to leave him behind?

"You are a queen," Daman snarled as he lifted his hands to her shoulders. "And a queen does not have to choose."

He yanked the sleeves of her tunic down, baring her breasts in the pale moonlight. "Come touch," he ordered over her shoulder as he cupped her in the palms of his hands. As he rolled her nipples between his fingers, Ella sagged against him, but her eyes never left Cadeyrn.

"Come taste." When he licked her neck, Ella moaned, her eyes now half lidded with desire.

"Come claim," the fae growled as he sank his teeth into her shoulder.

Crying out in pleasure and pain, Ella lifted a hand up to hold Daman close. "Cadeyrn," she breathed, needing him to join them. She ached for his touch alongside Daman's, desired his cock between her legs as the fae took her mouth.

"*Cadeyrn,*" she begged.

He hesitated for another second. But then he was striding towards her, his eyes dark with arousal, his cock hard with need. She'd watched it twitch under Daman's words, watched it grow under his caressing of her body.

"Ella," Cadeyrn rasped as he stopped in front of her. His eyes dipped to her breasts, both held up in offering by Daman. He reached out a hand, trailing his knuckles gently across her chest.

"Kiss me," she breathed.

The two of them eagerly obliged.

Chapter Nine

The Choice of a Queen

Cadeyrn kissed her gently, reverently. He cherished her while Daman marked her neck like an animal. His tongue swept across her lips, asking instead of demanding. Daman's teeth scraped across her skin, claiming without permission. The contrast of their skills left Ella trembling between them.

She parted her lips, pushed her tongue into Cadeyrn's mouth. He hissed. She moaned. And Daman reached up to grab her chin. He wrenched her head towards him and captured her lips with his own. Greedy and demanding. Animalistic and controlling.

Opening her eyes, Ella tried to catch Cadeyrn's gaze, but he was already lowering his head. Daman offered him one of her breasts and Cadeyrn licked around his fingers.

Sagging back on a gasp, Ella's eyes fluttered close. Cadeyrn lavished her breast with his tongue and his lips. He sucked on her nipple, coaxing it to erection.

Feeling behind her, Ella searched for Daman's cock. She wrapped her fingers around its hard length, marveled at its length and thick girth. He rocked against her, pushing his cock further into her fist.

Releasing her lips, Daman kissed along her jaw. He left love marks down her neck, across her shoulders. He squeezed the breast Cadeyrn wasn't focused on, pinching her bud between his fingers before letting it go and trailing his fingers south. He grazed across her stomach as his lips came back to her mouth. He parted her legs and stroked her until she was moaning so loudly she couldn't hear the birds anymore.

Cadeyrn growled, the noise vibrating across her nipple. He moved to her other breast as he too lowered a hand to the junction between her legs. Ella jerked, spasming on a wave of pleasure before either of them had even gone inside her. She threaded her fingers through Cadeyrn's hair, holding him close as she continued to stroke Daman's cock behind her.

"Please…" she begged against Daman's lips. He lifted his head. Looking into her eyes, he thrust a finger inside her.

Cadeyrn had done it at the same time and together they took her over the edge of sanity. On a scream of pleasure, Ella sagged forward. Cadeyrn pushed her upright and Daman held her with his other hand. Neither of them removed their fingers. Neither of them stopped giving her pleasure.

With his other arm wrapped around her, his palm on her breast, Daman bit her shoulder. Cadeyrn licked her nipple, then kissed the underside of her other breast. He trailed his lips lower, bent down until he was on his knees. His breath left goosebumps along her skin.

Ella sucked in a breath as she looked down. His head was level with their hands. She trembled. Her eyes half lidded with desire, Ella wound her fingers through Cadeyrn's hair and tugged him closer. He moved easily, as eager to please her as she was to feel his lips on her sensitive flesh.

His tongue was like nothing she'd ever felt before. Throwing her head back, Ella cried out in ecstasy. Her eyes locked with Daman's. They were full of lust, dark and greedy and wanting her.

Reaching for him, Ella brought his mouth to hers. She kissed him with the same savagery he had her. Within half a second, he had taken control, dominating her like he did everything.

Removing his hand from her pussy, Daman lifted his head. Holding her gaze, he sucked on his soaked finger. Ella's nostrils flared as her mouth dropped open. Her swollen lips trembled with need, but instead of kissing her again, he moved to stand in front of her and lowered his head to her breasts.

Now free to set his own tempo, Cadeyrn slowed the pace of his finger inside her. He curled it at the end, hitting her just right to cause tremor after tremor to rock her off her feet.

Holding each of their heads to her, Ella moaned. She ground her hips against Cadeyrn's mouth while she arched into Daman's. They pushed her over the edge with their tongues and lips, but neither seem to notice. Neither of them stopped. Neither gave mercy to her uncontrollable tremors.

And then Daman was on his knees in front of her. She thought Cadeyrn would come up now, change places and kiss her breasts, her lips…

But instead they just shared her, taking turns tasting her, alternating between who gave pleasure and who watched. Their heads were so close together, their eyes so dark with arousal that Ella found herself wishing they would kiss. She wanted them to pleasure each other just like they were pleasuring her.

"Daman…"

He looked up, peering into her soul.

"Kiss him," she breathed.

Wrenching Cadeyrn towards him, the fae did as she'd demanded. Ella sucked in a ragged breath as she watched him thrust his tongue inside her friend's mouth. Cadeyrn froze for a second, two before he started kissing him back. Each of them fought for dominance, their tongues going back and forth until the fae won out. He pushed Cadeyrn to the ground, then tugged on Ella's wrist, guiding her down on top of him.

She sat on his face, a leg on either side. As Cadeyrn continued where he'd left off, both hands on her arse, Daman rose and stood in front of her. He gripped his cock with one hand. It pulsed with desire, a bead of precum already glistening in the moonlight.

Knowing what he wanted, Ella leaned forward. She took him as deep as she could, but he pushed even deeper. She started to choke, but he was already pulling out. Before she could take a good breath, he was ramming his cock back inside her.

Cadeyrn squeezed her arse as he brought her to the edge. One of his hands trailed lower. It wrapped around her thigh as a finger stroked her wet pussy. Then it trailed back along her crack…and pushed against her hole. She tried to scream, but her mouth was too full for sound to come out.

On a roar of passion, Daman exploded down her throat. Assaulted on both ends, Ella wiggled in an attempt to free herself, but Daman held her head pressed against his belly and Cadeyrn had one arm wrapped around her waist, holding her still. His finger pushed further inside her. His lips sucked on her vagina.

Thighs quivering, Ella fell forwards when Daman finally released her. His cock was still erect, still hard despite his recent orgasm.

Shakily, Ella wiped at her mouth with the back of her hand as she watched him walk behind her. He knelt over Cadeyrn's chest, mimicking her pose. Pulling her back against him, he kissed her shoulder. Claimed her lips.

Just as she started to relax, his hands gripped her arse. Trailed lower.

She jerked when he joined Cadeyrn's finger. She was already stretched too tight. She couldn't take –

Screaming, Ella fell forwards onto her hands. Cadeyrn released her waist to cup one of her swaying breasts. Wiggling beneath them, he inched up between her arms until he was face to face with her.

She looked into his lust-filled green eyes as Daman stroked her arse. Something thick and hard replaced their fingers. Squeezing her eyes shut, Ella began to tremble.

Cadeyrn stroked her cheek. He lifted his head and tenderly kissed her, momentarily distracting her from Daman's actions.

But then the fae was pushing inside her. He moved slowly, giving her time to adjust. There was a moment of pain and she clenched her jaw, her hands fisting on the ground.

And then it was gone, replaced by a pleasure that left her breathless.

Feeling her finally relax, Cadeyrn's kiss turned more savage, more desperate. Removing his hand from her cheek, he reached down to grab his cock. He rubbed it against her, trailing the end back and forth against her wet lips before pushing it inside.

Only once Cadeyrn was fully sheathed did Daman begin to move. He rocked forward, making her gasp in pleasure. Thrusting his hips upward, Cadeyrn began to match the fae's pace.

Grabbing her hair, Daman tugged upwards until she was straight on her knees. He pulled her head back and stared into her eyes as he pumped inside her arse.

Their breaths mixed as one before he took her lips in an upside down kiss.

Moaning, Ella closed her eyes. Her breaths came out faster, more erratic. On the verge of another release, she placed both hands on Cadeyrn's chest and picked up speed.

Cadeyrn came first, his fingers digging into her hips as he arched back, his eyes closed. As he shuddered inside her that triggered Ella's orgasm and she came on a wave of ecstasy. Growling against her open mouth, Daman swept his tongue inside her, pumped three more times, and then came on another roar.

Gasping, Ella fell forward. She had not the strength to stop her descent now that Daman had let her go. Cadeyrn's arms came around her as she trembled on his chest. He stroked her back tenderly.

Closing her eyes, Ella yawned. But even as she drifted off, they both started to move again...

Chapter Ten

The Stroke of Midnight

Ella stared into the flames, remembering Daman's words from the night before. It almost didn't seem real – any of it. If not for the hot looks Cadeyrn had kept shooting her, she might have thought it'd been a dream.

She'd awakened in the atrium, having been carried there by one of them. She would've preferred waking outside with them or at the very least, in Daman's guest room, but she understood why she hadn't. Flavia had never been one to share her toys.

And Aurelia, Ella recalled with a pang of jealousy. Even 'good-natured' Aurelia might wish to punish them had she known what they were doing last night.

Staring at the growing flames, Ella wondered if

Octavia would stake them to the bonfire if her daughters asked it of her. Although their domina had calmed over the years after her husband's death, she was not a nice master by any means. She worked them hard and offered few luxuries. And if they messed up or displeased her in any way, they were punished severely.

But worse of all, there was Flavia. Octavia had done nothing to rein in her monster of a daughter. Had done nothing to stop her from burying Fial with Marcellus.

Anger growing, Ella tried to reach out to the flames. They were only small though. The bonfire had only just been started. It wasn't even as big as the three sheep beside it yet.

As the animals bayed in fear, each tugged on their leads in a desperate attempt to escape. Looking at them, Ella wanted to free them, reminded too much of Fial's last moments, but sacrifices had to be made.

Today was Samhain, the day when Cailleach, the Queen of Winter, was reborn. The day when ghosts and other mythical beings could pass into this world. Beings like her.

A fire elementalist, Daman had called her. But how could that be true?

"Well, don't just stand there!" Flavia snapped as she came up behind her.

A whip cracked against Ella's back, causing her to stumble forward. She clenched her jaw, knowing better than to clench her fists.

Turning around, Ella bowed stiffly.

"Since ye like the flames so much, maybe I'll let you take their place," Flavia purred as she nodded at the three sheep. She coiled the whip in her hands. An ugly sneer matched her wicked eyes.

"Please, don't, d–"

"Please, don't, Domina!" Flavia spat as she snapped the whip across Ella's cheek.

Biting her tongue, Ella said, "Please, don't, Domina."

Flavia's sneer widened. She pretended to mull it over before saying, "No, I think I will. You have been such a *model* slave recently. I must reward you somehow… And being a sacrifice for a good harvest is – " she glanced at the three sheep – "all so very honourable."

All of Ella's colour drained from her face.

Delighted with herself, Flavia turned away with a skip in her step.

"A sacrifice…" Ella whispered in horror. Glancing at the sheep, a terrible dread tightened around her chest.

The sacrifices opened the festivals. They were needed to stop the ghosts and other nefarious spirits from wrecking the lands when the Otherworld got too close.

Ella hadn't mastered fire yet. She wasn't even able to make it do anything. Daman was supposed to show her how tonight. But if she was to be a sacrifice, she had only until midday in which to live.

Swallowing, Ella lifted her chin. She refused to spend her last few hours wallowing in hopelessness and self pity. She would go down fighting, regardless of whether she had the power to control fire or not.

With a last look at the sheep, Ella went into the woods to collect more firewood. Three other bonfires had to be prepped before the feast could begin. Then going inside the house, she went in search for the animal skins they were to wear for the opening dance.

She'd just grabbed the wolf one when Felix appeared behind her.

"I'm sorry I kept ye up so late," he said after a

pleasant greeting. "Did you sleep well?"

Forcing a smile, Ella nodded.

"Good." Clearing his throat, he said, "I heard there was going to be a dance tonight and I was wondering if you would –"

"Isn't dancing below one such as yerself?"

"I actually find dancing to be –"

"What are ye doing here?" she blurted.

He was taken aback by her outburst, but he answered nonetheless. "I was looking for ye, and Daman said–"

"I mean here. In Provincia Britannia. In Derventio. What are ye doing here?"

A weariness came over his eyes. Frowning, he said, "I'm here to defend the empire from the people up north."

"From *my* people?"

He studied her, trying to decipher what direction this conversation was going to go in.

"Have ye killed any of them?" Ella demanded. "Have ye killed a tall ginger lad with a scar across his cheek?"

Lips pursing, he shook his head slowly. "I don't recall meeting anyone fitting that description."

Her heart broke. "But ye have met others already?" she croaked.

Sighing, he ran a hand down his face. "Yes."

"So ye could have…" She trailed off, unable to bring herself to say it. She'd already lost so much. She couldn't also lose the hope that her brothers were really alive. That Daman had been mistaken. How could he possibly have known anyway?

Seeing her fears, Felix took a step forward. He reached out a hand before thinking better of it. "I'm sorry my being here has brought ye pain," he murmured. "I am trying to find a peaceful solution to the raiding. If we can't come to terms though, I'm planning on approaching my father about building a wall. Maybe if the Roman Empire is seen as being well defended, the northern tribes will be less likely to attack." He hesitated a moment before revealing, "We have given up trying to conquer the high fells, so as long as yer family doesn't attack, they will be safe."

"Ye promise?"

His lips twisted into an apologetic frown. "There aren't any promises in war."

She respected his honesty; she just didn't like it.

Hugging the wolf skins tighter against her chest, Ella murmured, "I have to go."

Felix moved in front of her. "Come with me," he said quickly.

"What?"

"Back to Rome. I can take you away from all this, not just free you as a slave, but save you from this war."

Her mouth dropped open. Disgust furrowed her brows. "And be on the side that's slaughtering my family?" She shook her head. "I am *here* because of ye! Because ye kept raiding the Selgovae until they were desperate! My father –"

She looked away, her chest heaving. For a moment, there was nothing but angry silence between them. He lifted a hand to her cheek, but when she flinched, he dropped it back to his side.

"I'm sorry," he said sincerely. "If I could have chosen my parents, I would have."

"And yet ye cannot."

"No," he whispered as he finally stepped to the side. "No, I cannot."

The hours passed way too quickly. Ella hadn't been able to find Cadeyrn nor Daman at all. Now dressed in her freshly washed furs, she stood beside two other slaves on the outskirts of town. As the main bonfire roared behind them, reminding her of what was to come, Ella searched the faces in the crowd before them. Flavia was there front and centre, alongside her mother, her black guard, Roman, and Felix. Aurelia though, was glaringly missing.

Ella could not help but wonder if she was off with Cadeyrn somewhere…

And where in the world was Daman?

She had given him her name. He should be here, ready to save her, ready to uphold his end of the bargain.

But as the dance began, he still hadn't arrived.

And as it ended, he was still missing.

Lifting her chin, Ella caught Flavia's eye. The woman sneered and then looked pointedly at the flames. They were as tall as the trees now and crackled menacingly.

"Oh, Cailleach, the Great Goddess of Winter!" one of the dancers cried. He was dressed as a deer, complete with antlers branching out above his head. "Have mercy on us this season as ye rise from your slumber tonight! Oh, Pomona, Goddess of Fruitful Abundance, continue to bless us with yer favour, allowing our crops to grow and our harvest to reap!"

He danced as he prayed, moving in an intricate series of steps that were far too advanced for Ella and the other slave.

As soon as he'd finished, in that split second he'd bowed his head, Flavia stepped forwards and cried, "Let the sacrifices be made!"

A cheer rose up from behind her. Ella's heart caught in her throat as she looked once more for Cadeyrn and Daman.

Cadeyrn caught her eye at the back of the crowd. Aurelia stood beside him, radiating with an afterglow that left her sick.

Ella was certain that even being burned alive could not compete with the pain she was now feeling. She'd known last night what being with Cadeyrn had entailed and yet, she'd still hoped…

After what they'd shared, Ella had hoped he'd stay hers. But she was only a slave. She could offer him nothing.

You are a queen. Daman's words echoed in her head, but instead of resonating with power as they had last night, now they only mocked her.

A queen that was about to die. Burned in a sacrifice to a god that had never listened.

"And this year," Flavia continued as she turned to face the crowd. "In honour of Felix, the son of Hadrian and heir to the Roman Empire, we give thee a sacrifice like no other. We offer the three dancers!" she said with a flourish of her arm behind her.

Another round of cheers went up.

Clenching her fists, Ella glared with white hot fury. Her eyes met Cadeyrn's as he started pushing through the crowd. Frantically, she shook her head, knowing that if he made a scene, he would not save her. All he'd do was get himself tossed onto the fire alongside her.

Scowling, Cadeyrn let Aurelia pull him back.

"I do not require such a lavish show," Felix tried as he turned to Octavia. His voice was nothing but polite, but there was a tightness around his eyes.

I will be your champion.

Remembering his words, hope fluttered inside Ella's chest.

Then it died a quick and brutal death.

Whatever Octavia had whispered in his ear had caused Felix to close his eyes in regret. It seemed even the son of the empire had no clout when it came to the weight of Octavia's coin.

Clenching her fists, Ella felt the fire burning inside her. She tried calling to the flames, but like the gods, they did not hear her.

Walking towards her with a smug smile on her ugly face, Flavia sneered, "Tis a pity you'll be dying before tonight. I have plans to bring Cadeyrn into my bed again."

"Tell me," Ella growled since there was no need to force niceties anymore. "Does it bother ye that he thinks of Aurelia when he's inside you? That he prefers ye sister's cu–"

Flavia slapped her across the face. Her eyes burned so hotly, Ella knew she hadn't known about Cadeyrn and Aurelia.

Leering, Ella drove her words home. "He wasn't in ye bed last night, now was he? He was washing off ye stink before slipping between my –"

This one, she was ready for. Ella grabbed Flavia's wrist right before it'd connected with her face. Reaching behind her with her other hand, Ella removed the kitchen knife she'd hidden beneath her wolf skin. It'd cut into her back as she'd danced, but that was a small price to pay to have it now.

Sneering, she rammed the blade into Flavia's belly. She ripped it to the side, delighting in the feel of her domina's organs slicing clean in half.

Eyes wide, Flavia looked at her in shock. Her mouth fell open. Screams rose up behind her, but Ella did not care. She was already dead. At least she'd be taking this bitch with her.

"It's a slow death, a knife to the stomach," Ella purred. "Ye will still be able to watch me burn, aye, but ye will not be living long after I." She'd yelled that last bit, having been hauled away by Roman. She tried to stab his arm, but he was a warrior and easily knocked the knife out of her grasp.

"Throw her onto the fire!" Octavia screamed as she folded herself around her dying daughter. She cradled Flavia's head to her chest, whispering sweet words against her hair.

As Ella watched the blood seep into Octavia's tunic, she felt a moment of pity. Whatever slave would be tasked with removing the stains was going to have one bitch of a task.

Forced onto one of the wooden pyres, Ella lifted her eyes to the sky. She cursed the gods, not knowing that this time she actually had a celestial audience. Delentia, the Incarnation of Madness, smiled from afar. Her bat-like wings rumpled behind her as she rubbed her bony, little hands.

"Ye will all burn!" Ella screamed as Roman tied her to the stake in the middle. "I'll come back to kill ye children and destroy ye crops every Samhain!"

A torch was held at the bottom of her pyre. As the fire began to rise, Ella caught Cadeyrn's gaze. Silent tears fell down his cheeks, but he hadn't moved from his spot at the back. Aurelia still clung to him too as if she was offering him her strength.

Ella scoffed, her heart breaking. It seemed it wasn't just Cadeyrn who was stupidly in love. Aurelia was too, having chosen to comfort him rather than her sister and mother.

Maybe, just maybe the two would find happiness now that she was gone.

Suddenly exhausted, Ella sagged against her post. The smoke burned her lungs. The fire licked just under her feet. All too soon they were searing her flesh and as the first scream erupted from her lips, Ella looked at Flavia.

The woman was lying pale and weak on the ground. Her blood soaked through her mother's tunic and into the earth. She could not be saved. She would die tonight, painfully and slowly.

A smile breaking out across her lips, Ella's screams turned into high-pitched laughter.

Chapter Eleven

Everything Burns

She wasn't sure when it had happened. Ella had been too busy laughing to realise it at the start and then she'd passed out, suffocating on the smoke. But as the flames on her pyre started to dwindle and her consciousness slowly returned, she found that the fire no longer hurt her.

Awed, she rubbed at her wrists. The rope binding her had dropped into a pile of broken bits and ash. The wood had splintered beneath her feet, leaving her curled up on top of a pile of charred remains. The crackle of the fire still licked all around her, but it was no longer the glory it had been under the midday sun.

Under the light of the moon, Ella closed her eyes. She took a deep breath and tried to concentrate on the flames around her. She smiled when she felt them, laughed when she was able to control them.

A fire elementalist, Daman had called her. A queen.

Climbing to her feet, Ella walked through the flames.

She looked around the now empty field, the heat of vengeance burning in her heart. Everyone had long left this place, having retired to the centre of town in order to carry on with the festivities. Joy and laughter echoed through the night. But soon, they would be screams.

Lips curling, Ella took a step towards town. But at the feel of someone's presence behind her, she spun around and raised her fists.

Daman stood there with a tunic held out in front of him. There wasn't an ounce of regret nor shame on his face.

Ella's fists clenched with fury. The fire roared higher beside her, its flames now an eerie blue. A blue that unknowingly matched her eyes.

Grinning, the fae approached.

"I should kill ye for abandoning me," she snarled.

"Why?" he asked. "When it's because of me that you've risen a queen."

"Ye left me to burn alive!"

He looked down at her naked flesh. "And yet you have suffered no burns."

"I –" She stopped. Angrily, she grabbed the tunic he'd offered and put it on. "Ye promised to kill them, but I killed Flavia myself!"

"And I asked for your name, but I still do not have it."

"What are ye talking about? I told ye –" She stopped again as realisation grabbed her heart and twisted. "Are ye… Are ye saying me parents named me? That they loved me enough to name me? Then why…"

"Why had they abandoned you here?"

She nodded, not trusting herself to speak.

"I don't know, but we can find them and ask. Come with me, Fionnghula," he said as he held out his hand, "and together we can rule over Gaera, a world of prosperity and magic."

She was tempted. Oh, she was tempted, but first she had people to kill. She had told them they'd all burn one day and Ella wasn't willing to break her word.

"Ye played me," she gasped suddenly as she shoved at his chest. "Ye only want me for ye own gain!"

"When my goal matches your own, does it matter?" he asked flippantly. Threading his fingers through her hair, he yanked her head back. "And I did not play with you all the time. Last night for instance... I'd meant what I'd said. You are mine, Fionnghula."

Before she could protest, he crushed his lips to hers. He claimed her with his tongue, stroked the fire inside her until it was an inferno of desire.

Leaving her breathless, the fae lifted his head, but he did not step back. Looking into her eyes, Daman smiled. "And I am yours."

"I doona want ye," she spat.

He scoffed, his eyes mocking her as he looked at the erratic pulse in her neck.

"Go play, Fionnghula," he said in amusement. "But call for me when you're done."

And then he vanished right before her eyes.

Scowling, Ella walked into town, sparks flying from her fingertips.

The sound of buildings burning to the ground was only matched by the screams of Ella's victims. She walked from house to house, shop to shop, sparing no one from her wrath. Flames poured from her hands, fed by the fire inside her.

It wasn't until she saw Cadeyrn that the flames stopped. He stood with Aurelia, holding her in his arms as if he could protect her from the heat.

For a moment, Ella was tempted to burn Aurelia alive. He didn't need her anymore. Ella was no longer a slave and nor was he. She was freeing him tonight. Holding out her hand, Ella called to him.

"Cadeyrn, come with me and Daman! We are going to a new land where we will never be slaves again!"

He took a step forward, but Aurelia hugged him tighter. Stopping, he looked down into her upturned face. Tears lined her cheeks. Fear blazed in her eyes.

Ella frowned. "Cadeyrn…" she said uncertainly, but then she shook her head. Surely, he would not choose a Roman whore over her.

And yet he hesitated.

"Cadeyrn!" she cried.

He looked at her, pain in his eyes, and in that moment, Ella knew.

He had made his choice and it wasn't her.

Her shoulders bowed forward. The pain left her broken. She didn't understand. He was her everything. He was the only piece of her home she had left and she was his. They had been through so much together. But he'd chosen –

"*Why?*" She hadn't been able to stop the sound of her broken heart from escaping. What did Aurelia have that she didn't? He'd said he'd loved her. He'd said he'd loved her more than the bitch on his arm. "Why?" she screamed.

"I – "

Ella dropped to her knees on a gasp. Pain ruptured down her back and she was instantly reminded of her father's last moments. She looked over her shoulder, saw the arrow sticking out of her back. Just as she reached around to grab it, another one slammed into her. It was inches below the first.

Looking up with a growl, Ella spotted her enemy. *Octavia.*

The woman stood proudly, a bow in her hands. Eyes narrowing, she nocked another arrow in her string and drew it back. She aimed right for Ella's eyes.

Aurelia screamed. Cadeyrn shouted her name.

Burning with fury, Ella clenched her fist. A fireball formed in her hand. Spinning around, she chucked it at Octavia. It slammed into her chest at the same time the arrow flew. The projectile whizzed across her cheek, cutting the skin.

She smiled in triumph as Octavia came out worse. The fire licked at her tunic and her domina slapped at it wildly. But Ella's delight quickly faded when a scream erupted behind her.

It was feminine and panicked. Fearing for Cadeyrn's safety, Ella snapped back around. Her own cry tore from her chest as she looked at the blood pooling around his heart.

"Cadeyrn!"

Ignoring the pain her movement caused, Ella jumped to her feet. She rushed forward, but didn't make it in time to catch him.

Cadeyrn sagged to his knees, his eyes wide and glazed.

"Ella…"

"Cadeyrn!" She slid onto her knees, grasping his head in her hands. "Stay with me. Please!" Tears ran down in torrents. The fire around her roared a bright blue. Her pain was like nothing she'd ever felt before.

"Daman!" she screamed. "Daman, help!"

He appeared in an instant. Aurelia sucked in a breath, but she didn't intervene. Ella would have burned her alive if she had.

"Help him," she begged. "Please."

Daman knelt down beside her. He looked at her, but she refused to look away from Cadeyrn. His light was already fading. Clutching his hand, Ella brought it to her cheek. He didn't have the strength to hold her. His mouth opened and closed. His eyes glistened over.

"He's gone," Daman murmured softly.

"But ye can bring him back."

He shook his head. Placing a finger under her chin, he turned her to face him. "Even we do not have power over life and death."

"But the tales –"

"Are just tales." He wiped at her tears. "I would bring him back for you if I could."

Pulling her against him, Daman held her close. Then he pulled her to her feet, ripping her away from Cadeyrn. She wanted to punish him for that, but he turned her around and nodded. "Octavia's still alive."

The woman had put out the fire and was struggling to her feet.

For a moment, Ella didn't care. She just wanted to grieve. And then she saw the bow. Her fury roaring back to the forefront, Ella stalked forward. Fire formed in her palms. "Ye killed him!" she screamed as a circle of her pain and fury erupted into flames around Octavia.

"It was your fire that did it," Octavia pointed out as she rose to her feet. She held her chin high, leering over her as always. "You burned the feathers. You moved out of its way, knowing he was behind you. You killed him, Ella, just as you killed my husband."

"Ye husband was a monster!" Ella spat. "Doona dare compare the two!"

"Marcellus needed help."

"He *needed* to stop being provided little children!" The fire blazed hotter, its colour turning a depressing blue.

"I did what any mother would do!" Octavia shot back. "I protected my children at *whatever* the cost!"

"Tell that to the gods," Ella snarled. She didn't care about Octavia's reasoning. She had suffered greatly at this woman's hands for nearly a decade. The least her domina could do was die screaming in pain.

Forming a ball of fire in her palm, Ella took aim. But then she stopped.

Snuffing out the flames, she purred, "Thank ye, Domina, for teaching me the art of pain."

Looking at Daman, Ella demanded, "Grab Aurelia."

"No!" Octavia lunged forward, but the line of fire roared higher. It grabbed at her, seeking her flesh under Ella's command. Screaming, Octavia fell back and slapped at the flames on her tunic. "Leave her alone!" she cried. "Aurelia has never harmed you! Kill me, but –"

"She stole Cadeyrn!" Ella screamed. "She seduced him away from me! I was trying to save him! Save him from you! This is your doing, Octavia, and now it is time for you to feel my pain!"

Snarling, Ella threw a ball of fire at Octavia. She let it burn the woman's face, but stopped it from taking her eyes. She wanted Octavia to watch her daughter suffer. She wanted her to beg the gods for mercy before knowing what it felt like to be ignored.

"Then kill me!" Octavia screamed.

"And grant ye a mercy ye never gave me?" Ella snorted as she snuffed out the flames on her face.

Bright red blisters marred Octavia's cheeks. Her hair was singed completely. Only her eyes looked as they used to.

Aurelia was shoved to the ground in front of Ella's feet. Daman towered over her, his darkness matching Ella's own.

Forming a ball of fire, Ella directed it at Aurelia's legs. She would burn the woman from the bottom up, inch by inch, dragging it out all night if she could.

"She's pregnant with his child!" Octavia shouted.

The flames disappeared from Ella's hands. "Ye are lying," she said automatically, but her voice wavered with uncertainty.

Aurelia had placed her hands over her belly when Daman had pushed her to the ground. They were still there now, protectively hugging her middle.

"Is it true?" Ella demanded as she looked at Cadeyrn's lover.

"Yes..." Aurelia said, choking on her tears.

"Is it..." Ella swallowed. "Is it Cadeyrn's?"

She nodded and Ella didn't know whether to scream or cry. Cadeyrn might have passed into the Otherworld, but a part of him still lived on. Unless she killed Aurelia...

Looking at Octavia, Ella felt a part of the fire inside her start to die. She would take her revenge, but not by killing Cadeyrn's child.

"Ye will name it after him," Ella declared. "Ye will tell it of its father's greatness. Ye will not let him be forgotten. Do ye understand?"

The woman nodded, tears running down her cheeks. "I loved him. I won't ever forget him."

"Make sure ye don't or I will kill ye like I'm about to kill ye mother."

Her eyes holding Aurelia's, Ella formed a ball of fire in her palm. She increased its heat until the blaze turned a beautiful blue. Without breaking her gaze, she chucked the ball at Octavia.

It exploded on the woman's chest, consuming her as if she'd been covered in oil. Octavia's screams rang clear into the night. Concentrating hard, Ella kept the smoke from suffocating her old domina. She wanted Octavia to suffer for as long as possible. She wanted the bitch to burn.

Fighting back her tears, Ella grabbed Daman's hand. It was a silent acceptance of his offer to take her home.

The End

Epilogue

happily Never After

Daman smiled as he looked up at the sky. It was two minutes until midnight. Two minutes until the portal to Gaera was at its weakest. For millennia, he had been stuck here on this godsforsaken rock with these pestering humans as his only company. But now he was finally going to have his freedom. He was finally going home.

And then he was going to kill all of the fuckers that had trapped him here.

His jaw tightened. His eyes hardened as fury boiled inside him. Those bastards had taken everything from him. They had made it so *Adam fucking Dullahan* had been able to usurp his throne. That man was a coward and a weakling, unable to take him on an equal field.

Every day, Daman had prayed that Adam was still alive. For when he finally made it home, he wanted the pleasure of killing the bastard himself.

Furious even after all these years, Daman's hands tightened into fists. The grass withered at his feet. The flowers wilted. Clenching his jaw, he forced himself to relax. The vegetation grew back again, greener and healthier than before.

Soon, he growled. *Soon, I'll be able to go home.*

And he didn't mean to that damn circle of stones he'd been forced to live in for the last fifteen hundred years either. No, soon he would be relaxing in his castle on Gaera with Adam's screams echoing through his walls.

As Ella shifted in her sleep on the grass beside him, Daman smiled.

And then he frowned.

He was growing too attached to her. He was supposed to use her and leave her. That had been Delentia's terms. The goddess wanted Ella for her own purposes, and as powerful as Daman was, he wouldn't stand a chance against her.

"Thinking of running away with her?" a high-pitched voice sang from the shadows.

Rising from his perch on the grass, Daman frowned. "Of course not," he assured the goddess.

She was a small thing, barely coming up to his waist. Her skin was blood red. Two leathery, horned-tipped wings sprouted from her back. Checkered loincloths barely covered her privates. A cloak made of blue reptile skin was draped across her bony shoulders. Batting her long lashes, Delentia smiled up at him. A row of pointy teeth flashed between her lips.

"A pity. I do love a hunt." She tsked. "But take things

too far once with some guy's penis and no one ever wants to chance your wrath again." Rolling her eyes, she sighed. "Seriously though. It's a penis, a lump of flesh that dangles between your legs. What's your guys' big attachment to it?" She snorted. "Well, not big. It was actually pretty small." Raising her hand, she wiggled her pinkie.

"I've held up my end of the bargain," Daman said curtly. He wasn't in the mood for Delentia's ramblings.

The goddess' eyes narrowed. "Gee. Someone is in a surly mood. It's because of her, isn't it? You fucked her, didn't you?" Scowling, she placed her hands on her hips. "What did I fucking say about keeping your cock out of her vagina?" Her eyes suddenly glazed over as she looked into a timeline he couldn't see. Grinning, she snapped back to the present and shook her head. "Why you sly little cat. I guess you technically followed the rules, after all."

Clenching his jaw, Daman struggled to hold onto his patience.

"Fine," Delentia sighed. As she snapped her fingers, a portal opened behind her. "Let's go before you turn even more moody. Although…" Her eyes crinkled. A sly smile formed at her lips. "If you took her and ran, you do have a hundred percent chance of escaping me for ninety-nine percent of the time you'd have left to live."

His eyes narrowed. She meant she'd kill them in an instant. "Gods, you are such a bitch."

Delentia grinned as she shrugged one shoulder. "Praise, my dear, will get you nowhere."

She turned on her heels and skipped to the portal. His homeworld shone through the other side of it, his dream for the last fifteen hundred years. Still, he hesitated, his gaze lingering on Ella.

Shaking his head, Daman steeled his resolve. This was ridiculous. He barely knew her. She meant nothing to him. He took a step forward.

And then he stopped.

Daman might not know everything that made her laugh or what things she loved, but he knew the one thing that mattered the most.

He knew that she was his.

Damn her.

"Delentia…" he said tightly, his gaze flicking back to Ella.

The goddess stopped on a sigh. Looking over her shoulder, she warned, "It will not be a life of happiness."

He thought about it for a second even though his heart had already made the decision. For fifteen hundred years he'd felt nothing.

And then he'd felt her.

Ella had touched parts of him he'd thought were long dead. When he'd watched her get dragged onto the pyre, he'd struggled not to kill everyone there. Only Delentia's foresight of Ella's survival had held him back.

But even still, he had not been able to keep his usual tight control. Roman had died by his hands soon after. As had Felix. He had not been able to leave that bastard alive after having heard him ask Ella to run away with him.

She was *his. Only* his.

As he watched her sleep, her brows still furrowed in pain over the loss of Cadeyrn, Daman growled, "I cannot leave her."

Delentia shrugged. "Then take her place and I'll spare her life."

She smiled brightly, not even bothering to pretend

that she was unhappy with the change in her plans. Eyes narrowing, Daman realised he'd been played. This had been Delentia's desire all along – to have him, a powerful dark fae, as her personal assassin.

Giggling, Delentia skipped into the portal. She didn't need to wait for his answer; she already knew what it would be.

And honestly, so did he.

Scowling, Daman strode towards Ella. He couldn't afford the weakness she inflicted upon him. As soon as he sated his fill, he would leave her, he assured himself.

But that was before he'd gathered her into his arms. Before she'd curled against his chest and relaxed on a sigh.

A heaviness settled inside him as he detailed her now peaceful face. His grip tightened around her. His eyes hardened. He would protect his queen regardless of what it cost him.

It might cost you everything, his brain whispered as he walked into the portal.

But his heart so easily replied.

So be it.

Thank you so much for making it to the end of this novella!

If you'd like to read more about Ella and Daman, sign up to my newsletter. Their story is far from over.

Sign me up now!
mirandagrant.ck.page/b05fb957b7 (direct)
mirandagrant.co.uk (sign-up form)

Author's Note:

Derventio was a real town occupied by the Romans. It was a military compound tasked with maintaining order inside of Cumbria, as well as offering support to Luguwalos (present-day Carlisle) when the Scottish invaded.

In 120AD, Derventio is actually believed to have suffered a massive fire. The site was then abandoned for over twenty years.

Felix did get 'his' wall in the end, the Scottish having had no desire to compromise on what was theirs. This was the beginning of the end for the Roman occupation in Britain. Even though they would linger around for another three hundred years, the Romans never had a prolonged time of peace with their Scottish neighbours.

The only real character in this story was Hadrian, the emperor whose name the England-Scotland wall retains.

xx Miranda Grant xx

PS: Keep turning for a sneak preview of The Little Morgen, book two of the Fairytales of the Myth.

Prologue

The Birth of a Monster
942, Sea of Darkness (Atlantic Ocean)

Thalliya swam through the deep blue sea, a smile stretching across her face. She flicked her tail faster and faster, gaining speed as she cut through the water like a dolphin. The sun shone high above her, its rays sinking into the dark depths of her home.

Angling up, she breached the surface and laughed. Her high-pitched giggle resonated in the hot morning air. Flopping backwards, Thalliya threw her arms out wide, allowing herself to float on top of the waves. The gentle lap of the water against her skin helped soothe the burn of the sun. She peered up at the sky, knowing better than to look at the bright yellow orb directly. The last time she'd done that, she hadn't been able to properly see for ages.

"Ta-ya!"

Smiling at the shout of her name, the little mermaid

dove back underwater. She waved at her baby brother as he swam towards her. His blue and white striped tail cut through the water with a smoothness that belied his usual clumsiness.

"Ketea!" she gushed, her eyes shining brightly.

Her little brother smiled widely. Racing towards him, Thalliya grabbed his arm and dragged him backwards. He squealed in pure delight, loving the speed at which she swam.

Looking up, Thalliya spotted the rest of her family. Her twin sister vibrated with the same excited energy as she did. Her mother and father both smiled warmly as their dark blue tails propelled them forward.

"Are you ready? I'm so excited!" her twin gushed as she swam towards Thalliya. "I can't wait to wiggle my toes. Ariel said we get ten of them. Ten!"

"I –"

"And I want to move through the humans' portals. All of them. Ariel says you have to learn the right magic first, but she said a guy-she-spoke-to-there's buddy absolutely said it was possible to do. Like for anyone. Even for you and me. Don't you want to learn magic?"

"Marina," their mother said with a small chuckle.

Turning with wide eyes, she looked at their parents. "Did you learn magic when you went to land?"

"It's not magic; it's something they call reading."

"Reading magic?"

"No, it's –" She stopped as she shared a loving look with their father. "Yes, reading magic."

"I can't wait!"

Neither could Thalliya. She'd dreamed of walking on land every night for the last year. She was finally of age. In another few minutes, she'd feel what it was like to have legs!

"Hey, doofus!"

Their father rolled his eyes before turning to face his brother, who was also their king. Ariel waved at them from beside him. Thalliya and Marina waved back.

"You heading off?" their father asked.

The king nodded. "Ariel has a recital at two." Turning to face her and Marina, he smiled. "Make sure you try this thing called honey. It's delicious."

Her sister nodded enthusiastically, her eyes practically popping out of her head. Thalliya giggled. Sharing a glance with her twin, she silently agreed not to say anything. The faster this conversation was over, the faster they could get their legs.

Laughing, their uncle shook his head. "Okay, okay. We're off. You two be good." As he swam away, he shouted over his shoulder, "And don't forget about the honey!"

She wouldn't.

Eyes shining, Thalliya grabbed her sister's hand and dragged her through the water. Laughing, their parents followed suit, holding Ketea between them.

"The last one to Malaqah is a rotten crab!" Releasing her twin's hand, Thalliya swam as fast as she could.

But Marina was faster. She blitzed through the water like a dolphin, sticking her tongue out as she passed. Showing off, she turned around and swam backwards.

Thalliya's eyes narrowed. As much as she'd practised that manoeuvre, she'd yet to accomplish it. She was just about to stick her own tongue out when her mother screamed behind her.

"*Stop*!"

Startled, Thalliya did as she was instructed. She turned

to look back at her parents. Her mother's face was pale; her father's was full of horror. As they raced towards her, Thalliya opened her mouth to ask what was wrong. But she didn't get the chance.

Ketea was thrust into her arms.

"Stay here!" her mother shouted.

She turned, watching them swim ahead. Her mouth was still open. Her brain was still frozen with confusion.

But then Marina screamed and Thalliya's blood ran cold as she finally registered what she was seeing. She clutched Ketea to her chest as she started to shake. Her twin was entangled in a net that was being wrenched to the surface.

Not knowing what to do, Thalliya stayed where she was. And she hated herself for it.

"Hold on, Marina!" their mother shouted.

"We're coming for you!"

"Mother!" She reached out a hand as their father made it to her side.

"Marina!"

"Help!"

Thalliya turned Ketea's head against her chest, holding her hand over his eyes. She wanted to cover her own, but she couldn't.

She watched as Marina was dragged upwards by the fishing net. Their mother held her hands, trying to pull her free. Their father grabbed the bottom of the net and tried to swim down. Neither were of any use. Marina disappeared above the surface. And her mother was wrenched up too.

Thalliya gasped. Trembling, she backed away. What could she do? What could she do?

"Father!"

"Stay there!" he ordered as he swam for the surface. His dark blue tail cut through the water like a knife. His anger, his fear, they were near palpable. And then, he too was gone, wrenched above the surface by another net.

She watched him go over the side of a ship. A dragon-head was carved into the bow, its fearsome teeth on full display. As the joyful shouts of men assaulted her, the ship rocked above her head. Another net was tossed into the water…and then wrenched back up empty.

Her heart thudded in her ears like crashing waves.

"Ta-ya!"

"It's okay," she cried. "It's going to be okay." Holding him close, she started to swim for the surface. She just needed to look, to see that her sister and mother and father were okay. She just needed to –

She screamed.

A shape had been unceremoniously dumped back into the water. Blood spread everywhere. She knew it was one of them, but she didn't know who. The person's tail and fins were gone. And so was their head.

Shuddering, she brought both hands to her eyes. But she couldn't turn away. She couldn't stop herself from peeking out between her fingers. Another body hit the water. Wrapping her arms around her waist, she held herself like she wished her mother or her father would.

A third body was dropped, this one smaller. Her size. She screamed and screamed. Swishing her tail, Thalliya propelled herself forward. It was only when she caught another movement out of her eye, that she realised she'd let go of Ketea.

Her heart stopped.

Her tail froze.

Her mouth opened and closed uselessly as she

watched him swim towards one of the bodies.

She needed to get to him. She needed to grab him before the humans did. She'd thought they were friendly. No one had told her they could be this cruel. But even though she knew what she should do, she couldn't move.

Fear left her frozen. She tried to call out to him, to beg him to come back.

But she was too late. A net came down and scooped him up.

He was gone. Just like all the others.

Trembling, Thalliya shook her head. This couldn't be happening. It *couldn't*. She prayed, despite all evidence, that this was just a dream. That she would wake up and everything would be okay. That *everyone* would be okay. "Don't leave me!"

She shuddered with every intake of breath. This was supposed to be a day of happiness, of excitement. She and Marina were supposed to be trying honey right now. She couldn't…

No…

This couldn't…

Swimming towards her twin, she screamed. *"No! Noooooooo!"* She pulled Marina's body against her and rocked her back and forth as another splash reached her ears. She refused to look up, refused to see what she knew in her heart to be true. "Sis, *please! Please…*" she cried.

She heaved so hard, her chest hurt. But she couldn't stop. She couldn't stop.

Her stomach revolted. Her pain increased.

"Marina…"

She cried until she couldn't see anymore due to the puffiness of her cheeks. Until her devastation turned into anger. Into rage.

Squeezing her sister's hand, Thalliya lifted her head and howled.

"Quiet ye screams, my child." The words were said as a murmur and yet, they slid into Thalliya's head at a volume that was impossible to ignore.

Startled, she stopped crying. Forcing her eyes open, she stared at the woman before her. Her lips parted in awe.

The woman had legs.

And yet she floated in the water. Able to breathe. Able to speak.

"Who are you?" Thalliya whispered.

The woman smiled. Her golden hair flowed around her, framing her beautiful face. "I am Freya Goddess of Love and War. I heard the pain in yer heart, my child, and I am here to offer ye the power to avenge yer family, should ye want it."

Thalliya's lip trembled. She nodded. She wanted that. She wanted that so much. Looking down at her sister, she murmured her name with barely a sound. "I want it."

"Then let her go. Give her to Ran so that ye may be mine."

Thalliya shook her head. She couldn't.

She *couldn't*.

"It must be done, my child. Ye cannot revenge her otherwise. Or Ketea. Or yer mother and father. Give her to Ran."

With a broken sob, Thalliya gripped her tighter. Then she kissed her chest, murmured an apology, and released her. She watched as her twin's body sank into the darkness. Gone forever.

"Tell me," she said, looking up. "Tell me how to

avenge them."

The goddess smiled as she held out her hand. "Give me yer heart, my child."

Thalliya frowned in confusion. "But I'll die."

"Nay. Ye will be reborn as my champion. With me as the keeper of yer heart, no one will be able to harm ye ever again."

Thalliya wanted to believe her. *Needed* to believe her. Otherwise, she'd have nothing worth living for. Her entire family was gone. She was all alone with just their screams for company. She couldn't live like this. A tear slid down her cheek before vanishing as just another drop in the ocean.

Trembling, she raised her chin. "Tell me how."

A golden comb appeared in the goddess' outstretched hand. Its handle was a mound of green and blue jewels. A sea dragon curled around them, guarding its treasure with a fierceness that stole Thalliya's breath. Beneath the dragon, three large teeth made up the bottom of the comb. Each one was sharpened to a deadly point.

Her heart pounded in her ears. With a hard swallow, she reached for the comb. It was hot to the touch, nearly scolding. She wanted to jerk her hand away, but she didn't dare. She wrapped her fingers around the dragon. Her eyes widened when it moved beneath her hand and bit her.

Had it not been for Freya, she would've dropped the comb. The goddess' hand closed over hers, forcing her to hold onto it as the sea dragon dug into the flesh of her palm. Thalliya's tail thrashed beneath her as tears stole her vision.

"It must feed on yer pain, my child."

"It hurts!"

"It will pass."

Crying out in agony, Thalliya tightened her fist around the comb. A large cloud of blood seeped from her hand. The dragon bit deep into her palm, chewing out a hole in the centre. And then it was inside her, moving up her arm.

Thalliya's screams increased in pitch and volume as she watched it slither beneath her skin. Every length it travelled, it did so by chewing the muscles and tendons in its way. By the time it reached her shoulder, Thalliya was shivering with convulsions.

But the pain she had just experienced was nothing compared to the agony she felt now as it slid across her ribcage and into her heart.

Throwing her head back, Thalliya screamed again.

"Do it now!" Freya shouted as she pushed Thalliya's hand towards her chest. The teeth of the comb scraped over her heart but did not break the skin.

Shaking violently from the pain, Thalliya didn't know if she could go through with it. It hurt so much already. She just wanted it to stop.

"Now, my child!"

She sobbed uncontrollably. She couldn't breathe. Couldn't think. Closing her eyes, she wished she could find comfort in her mother's arms.

But she never would.

Because they'd taken her from her. They'd taken everyone.

On a broken scream, Thalliya slammed the comb into her chest.

She gasped. Her heart jerked against the three teeth. Her eyes snapped open as she sagged forwards in agony.

"Give it to me!"

Tightening her fist around the comb, Thalliya gritted her teeth and pulled. Tears flooded the sea. She stopped, unable to endure the pain.

But then the pounding in her ears was interrupted by another splash. And another and another until she was drowning in the sickening sound that would haunt her forever. Clenching her jaw, Thalliya took a deep breath.

And ripped her heart free.

The goddess took it without hesitation. A bright light flashed in front of her, but Thalliya was too weak to lift her head.

"Breathe, my child. The pain will be over soon."

A warm hand touched her shoulder. The dragon inside her chest wriggled where her heart had lain. She clenched her teeth, expecting more pain. Startled, she looked up as a delicious heat spread through her entire body.

"Our deal is done." The goddess smiled warmly. Then her eyes hardened as she grabbed Thalliya's chin. "Never give yer heart to another," she warned, "or I will take back what I have just given."

Her lips trembling, Thalliya nodded. "Never," she whispered. Her fists opened and then clenched again. She would not rest. She would never know love.

Not until every last man was dead.

Elemental Claim

For him, the mission always comes first.

Rogan knows better than anyone what happens when a mission fails. Hundreds die, including those he'd sworn to protect. And this time, there are billions of lives hanging in the balance.

So he can't get distracted by the soft lips of his captive. And he damn well needs to resist the beckoning of his soul. For using Emma is the only way to find Sebastian the Ancient Destroyer, a sadistic vampire with plans to kill them all.

But for her, it's family.

Emma gets needing to save the worlds and everything. She really does. But Rogan wants, at best, to imprison her sister. At worst, to kill her. And with both parents already dead, Emma refuses to give up on the last of her kin.

Even if Elizabeth is now a mass murderer…

And she's willingly helping a monster…

Because family comes first.
Right?

Think Of Me Demon

Matakyli is a demon warrior princess and one of the guardians to the backdoor of Niflhel. Her death could lead to the dead escaping, potentially bringing about the annihilation of the Seven Planes. So when a prophecy claims that she will die by the hands of an ancient vampire, she and her brothers do all they can to change her fate. But there's only one solution.

For her to live, her lifemate has to die.

Only Galvanor isn't willing to be led like a lamb to slaughter. He's still suffering from his last visit to hell and isn't keen on returning, especially not for another woman.

But it's in Matakyli's nature to play with fire and enjoy the heat of its flames.

As she digs into the secrets he wants to keep buried, she discovers a soul worth saving.

But is his worth the cost of her own?

Tricked Into It

**The gods want him dead...
And so does his mate.**

The blood moon is rising. Werewolves are being forced to change. His teammates are being ripped apart by a sadistic vampire, their screams tearing through the night. Jack's role is simple. Grab the package, chuck it into the portal, and come back to cover his team.

Except that 'package' hates Jack with every fiber of her being. The first chance she gets, Charlie attacks him with a branch, kicks him while he's down, and spits in his face for good measure. She wants him dead, gone, and six feet under. At this point Jack wants the same.

But there's only one problem. Jack has a beast inside him. And it's just claimed Charlie as its mate.

Rage for Her

In the wrong hands, she'd be a weapon.

Phoebe has the power to make people act on their darkest desires, their sickest secrets. Sebastian wants to use her. The Royal Court wants to imprison her. And her lifemate wants to never see her again. It's been twenty years since he locked her away in an ivory tower and then crushed her heart under his heel. She wants to move on. Needs to move on…

But in Tegan's arms, she's just a woman.

Walking away from Phoebe was the hardest thing he ever did. When life gives him a second chance to see her again, Tegan refuses to let her go. But how does he woo a woman he no longer knows? And how in Hel's name does he keep her safe? Because the same things he left her to protect her from are still out there, hunting him, hunting her…

Nowhere is safe.

Lightning Source UK Ltd.
Milton Keynes UK
UKHW010021271121
394655UK00005B/1320